BENEATH THE MOON
AND LONG DEAD STARS

Beneath the Moon and Long Dead Stars
Copyright © 2025 by Daniel Wallace

Library of Congress Cataloging-in-Publication Data

Names: Wallace, Daniel, 1959- author.
Title: Beneath the moon and long dead stars :
stories / Daniel Wallace.
Identifiers: LCCN 2024036353 (print) | LCCN 2024036354
(ebook) | ISBN 9781949344561 (paperback) |
ISBN 9781949344578 (ebook)
Subjects: LCGFT: Short stories.
Classification: LCC PS3573.A4256348 B46 2025 (print) | LCC
PS3573.A4256348 (ebook) | DDC 813/.54--dc23/eng/20240816
LC record available at https://lccn.loc.gov/2024036353
LC ebook record available at https://lccn.loc.gov/2024036354

This is a work of fiction. No identification with actual persons (living or deceased), places, buildings, and products is intended or should be inferred.

Published in the United States of America

Cover art: Lillian Bayley Hoover, *Suburban Night*, Oil on Panel, 2013
https://lillianhoover.com/
Author photo: Kate Medley
Book design: Spock and Associates

Published by
BULL CITY PRESS
1217 Odyssey Drive
Durham, NC 27713

www.BullCityPress.com

CONTENTS

For Abby, Lillian, and Henry, who used to be small

THE PERFECT NAME

How close he had come to saying that he really hadn't had the puppy very long anyway, that it hadn't had a chance to burrow deeply into his heart, that he had only just started changing his entire life to accommodate it, to locate the dog parks, obedience schools, walking trails; that he had only just now begun experimenting with different kinds of dog food to find out whether he was a beef, chicken, or lamb dog, and if he liked to fetch. Some dogs liked to fetch, some didn't, and the jury was still out on this one. He didn't tell her that he had rearranged his bedroom, angling his bed against the far wall, in order to make room for the dog's crate, the portable metal jail the dog stayed in while he was at work. Not the whole day, of course. He'd come home from the office at lunch and let him out for a few minutes, and on very nice days he'd set the crate on the back porch, for no other reason than to give the dog a steady helping of fresh air, and to impress upon him the sense that his life extended beyond his owner's modestly crummy apartment. On one such lovely day he must have failed to hitch the latch securely. This is what must have happened, as he tried to reconstruct the events that led to this. It was that simple, the difference between all things: an unhitched latch. He had nosed the door open and dashed out into a world he would have no reason to believe wasn't his, a world where the only thing he really knew—his person—was out there somewhere, waiting for him to come. How he must have looked everywhere, through the yards, the parking lots, and finally the main road, so busy on toward evening. She was so sorry, she said, and she was, he could tell. It wasn't her fault. So he didn't tell her much of anything. But when asked what the dog's name was, he did tell her, reluctantly—or maybe it was his own reluctant self he was telling—how he had only just settled on one. That day in fact. It had come to him in a dream. He told her how he thought it was the perfect name for him, and, though she hadn't really known the dog, had only been there at the most important moment of its life, she said she was sure it was.

ALWAYS

They went out for a coffee and talked and laughed and two nights later went out for dinner and the food was terrible, the waiter was an asshole but they had the best time, the best, and the next night they were thinking about a movie but went to her apartment instead, where they had a massively wonderful night in bed. The sex was daily after that for weeks, at night and in the morning, random afternoon hookups when she would summon him via text while he was working. This was new to him. He stumbled through the day half-numb, the other half on fire, his brain filled with cobwebs. He felt like he had traveled to an exotic foreign country, a place where only two people lived, she and him, and they were having sex in it all the time and they were exhausted and their lips were raw, bruised from kissing long and hard. The sex was so good he wanted to tell his friends about it, his coworkers, he wanted to tell his parents: everybody would be happy for him. Just out of college, interning for a software start-up, and now this.

Her name was Marney.

He loved her name.

She was smart, funny. All that. Pretty too. He caught himself mooning over her sometimes, starstruck. And the sex. The sex.

Three weeks into it they had a conversation. They were in bed staring at the ceiling, a sheet draped across their chests. She said, out of nowhere, laughing before she said it, "It always starts off like this with me. With a bang."

He let that sit there for a second. "What do mean?" he said. "'Always.'"

"What?"

"What do you mean. *Always*."

She shrugged. "Nothing. Just that this is the way it always seems to happen. With a bang and then—"

"It just—"

"Yeah."

He realized he was holding his breath, so he breathed. "Sure," he said. "It can't stay like this forever. We'd probably die. But when you say *always*—"

"It's like a character trait or something."

"But *always*. That implies it happens—I don't know—a lot."

"What happens?"

"This," he said. "Us."

"Oh." She considered it. Played with the idea for a second. "I don't mean *us*. We're not like anything. We're us."

"Right. But in general. Generically. You mean always

all the time when something *like* this happens. Just, 'always' sounds like . . . more than a little. When you put it that way."

"Not necessarily. Always doesn't *mean* a lot. Even if it only happened twice and I'd only done it twice that would be 'always.'"

"So this is . . . the second time?"

"I didn't say that."

"So—"

He had one thought then, one thought, a series of words he focused on with every ounce of his being. It served as his mantra for the next half a minute or so: *Don't ask how many don't ask how many don't ask how many don't ask how many don't ask how many don't ask how many don't ask how many don't ask how many don't ask how many don't ask how many.*

"How many?"

"I knew you were going to ask me that."

They lay there quietly for a little bit longer. "How? How did you know?" he said.

"Know what?"

"That I was going to ask you that."

"Because. They always do."

It was getting so much worse.

"I withdraw the question," he said.

"You can't withdraw the question. This isn't like a court of law."

"Then what is it?"

"*What?*" She almost screamed at him. She really almost screamed. "What is what?"

"This. Here. What we are. Now. Whatever. What is it? What do you want it to be? Tomorrow, the next day, in a week, a year. What?"

He hadn't looked at her while they were talking, he couldn't, staring instead at a hairline crack in her ceiling, and the water spots on either side of it, a leak from the toilet in the apartment upstairs, perhaps? He had never noticed it before. It looked like an alien spaceship or a cheeseburger. Now he looked at her, though. He stared, the forlorn lover, at her silhouette. She was sad, he could tell so easily she was sad, the way her beautiful, heart-shaped face looked frozen, as if it had never smiled and never would. She was far away from him now, and somehow seemed to be drifting farther and farther as he looked at her. But God, she was beautiful, even in despair. She was like a sculpture, really, a work of art. He had never been with anyone as beautiful as Marney and as smart and funny as her and if something happened to the two of them he knew he was never going to be with someone quite so beautiful and smart and funny again. Close, maybe. But close is not nearly close enough. She must have felt him looking at her, must have. But she wouldn't look at him; she was doing her best to pretend he wasn't there. Finally, she slipped out from under the sheet and sat on the side of the bed with her naked back to him. Long and thin and soft, pale in the gray light, maybe a little boyish with her hair the way she wore it, so short and brown, shoulder blades like a pair of sleeping eyes. She didn't move a muscle. She barely breathed. "You should probably go," she said, and she was right. He should go. He was just a visitor here, after all, a tourist, the guy who does the thing that all the tourists do: sees the ruins, then goes home.

MENDING FENCES: THE MOVIE

I bought a car from one of those grassy roadside lots, paid in cash that arguably wasn't mine, and disappeared into the night like the smoky tail of a dying match. I was in the next state by morning, at a Waffle Shoppe full of truckers and farmers, all of them wearing baseball caps, none of them backward. I turned mine around.

I found a booth in the back. Waitress caught my eye and winked. "Be right with you, hon," she said, same as they always do, like it's from the handbook. Tangerine lipstick and penciled-in eyebrows, thin, tinsel-gray hair in a ponytail. She was my age probably but looked twice that, weary but indestructible, like she'd been standing up her entire life and would be buried that way too. She walked over to me with the pot, veins like river maps beneath her skin, face that had been through a lot, too much, but she smiled with a warmth that was so real I felt it in my heart. Nametag: *Kate*.

"Morning, baby. Coffee?"

I nodded, she poured. "What can I do you for, sweetie?" Like she might take me in her arms and rock me to sleep.

I kept my face low reading from the menu but when I looked up to order her eyes were fixed on me. She blinked once, kept staring. I could see her tongue resting against the top of her bottom teeth, her mouth hanging open just that much.

"Good lord." She gave me the once over twice. "You're—aren't you—?"

I turned away. There was a TV on the wall and I wondered if I'd been on it already, but nothing I'd done would make the news. That's what I told myself. I thought I was faster than my past. But maybe nobody is that fast.

She pointed at me.

"You're Dustin—Dustin—lord, my brain has gone to mush. I *just* saw you."

Impossible. Never in my life. And I'm no Dustin. "Sorry?"

"Last night. The movie, your movie. Oh, you know—*San Francisco Nights*! With Julia Roberts!" An exclamation point, like she'd just won a prize. "Dustin Evers. You are Dustin Evers and I cannot freaking *believe* it. Oh good lord."

Her smile made her makeup flake a little and her lipstick crack.

I shook my head. "I think you have me confused with somebody else." Matter of fact, a little gruff, putting her off without pushing too hard.

But her eyes wouldn't let me go.

Dustin Evers, I thought.

Dustin Evers, the actor.

I couldn't see what she was seeing but I didn't want to get into it.

"You got me," I said.

I'd seen that movie too. A pastry chef and a fireman fall in love when her bakery burns down. I shrugged and almost smiled and she shivered like a woman about to freeze. She motioned a cohort over, a girl who might have been her daughter, twins basically, separated by twenty or thirty years.

"Lucy," she said, in a whisper. "Get over here. Look at this."

Lucy dragged herself over and looked at me with her dull, dead, sleepy eyes. "Hey, sugar," she said. Then to Kate: "What am I looking at?"

"You're looking at Dustin Evers," Kate said. "*San Francisco Nights?*"

Lucy took a minute to fall into the magical world Kate made for her and just like that she was all in. She opened her mouth but no words came out.

"Oh, oh, oh wow," she said, finally. "Wow wow wow." Then, blushing: "I've had a crush on you since I was twelve."

They laughed. I laughed. Like I'd heard it all before.

"Well, thank you, I guess," I said. "The camera is kind to me."

"God was kind to you," Kate said. "That face of yours is a gift from God." She looked at Lucy and spoke as if I wasn't there. "I can't believe I'm saying this to Dustin Evers!"

"Dustin. Freaking. Evers."

"What's she like?" Lucy said. "Julia Roberts. They say she's nice but I think, I don't know, she might be full of herself."

I sipped my coffee and shook my head. "She's an absolute angel," I said.

"Is there a movie around here you're making?"

"Yes," I said. "There is. Right down the road."

"Wow," Lucy said. "Wow wow."

"That how you hurt your hand?"

She was addressing the blood lines on my knuckles.

"Yes. I do my own stunts."

"His own stunts."

Lucy and Kate. Did they ever have a story to tell now.

"What's it about?" Kate said.

"Yeah," Lucy said. "What's it all about?"

"What it's all about?" Philosophers now. "Well, I guess it's about a man who did some things he wished he hadn't done, tries to run away from it all, meets a woman on a farm who sees him for who he could be, deep down, then hires him on to mend fences, and they, well, you know."

"Sounds like my kind of movie. What's it called?"

"*Mending Fences*," I said, and I saw it unfolding before me. The woman on the farm—tall, copper hair, a widow maybe, tough, unyielding eyes at first but deep pools of goodness and almost spiritual power, me working the land for her, sleeping in the barn on a bale of old hay, her scraggly mutt my first best friend, that mutt follows me around everywhere, and I was milking cows, riding horses, saving her life from that snake—a rattler—that almost bit her, how we picnicked beneath that big old oak tree, the one her grandad planted a hundred years before, and then how one night we heard a pack of coyotes howling in the far fields and went to check on a heifer and chased those coyotes away, and I kissed her beneath a sickle moon, and finally I told her everything, everything I did leading up to the night I got that car from the roadside lot, all of it, I couldn't live that lie a minute longer but figured when I told her she would leave me and—she almost does. She almost leaves me but she doesn't, and she says to me, Hon, sweetheart, sugar, baby, damn it if I don't love you, but you gotta go back and make things right, you have to go back before we can move forward into whoever we're going to be, into the rest of our lives, together. And so in the movie I do, I go back and I see the girl who left me and I hurt the man she left me for and tell my mom and my dad how sorry I am for all the trouble I've caused them all of my troubled life and I do what I can to make it right, and then I come back to her and she takes me in her arms and the music swells and finally I'm happy, we're happy. "And that's why it's called *Mending Fences*," I said. I told them the whole thing, and by the time I was done I was surrounded by the truckers and the farmers, and a short order cook to boot. They loved Dustin so much. Someone even bought him breakfast. And then it was over. I told them I had to get back on set. But I want to thank the Academy and my amazing director and Julia for being the best costar a guy could ever ask for . . . But more than all of them put together I have to thank Kate and Lucy for that morning, for the greatest gift I ever got in my life, to be another man for just a few minutes, to be famous for not being me.

RAIN

We lived near the edge of a town near the edge of the sea, far away from the wide world. The town was called Rain. It was a place beyond the progress of most, but for others merely a point of departure: this was the common wisdom. Our house was the very last on the mainland, a lone brown stone cottage, slate-shingled with big picture windows on the sun sides, bright as change, the light as thick as butter all morning and afternoon. It was dark at night, though, so dark we were told that in the old days blind men worked as guides, but I don't think this was true. It was truly dark, though: the sea was not far, and at night the sea was even darker than the sky. Lovers and suicides from town walked past our house on their way to the cliffs: my father stayed up late nights reading, and they followed his light. Between the sound of the waves breaking below us, we could hear them tread the gravel in our drive—on their way, yes, but on their way to what we wouldn't know, not until the next day when someone's mother might come by weeping, throwing a bouquet of flowers off the cliffs into her child's wake.

The bodies of those who jumped were broken on the rocks directly below, swept out to sea with the tide and later washed ashore, horribly battered, on the islands to our west.

The people on the islands often complained, but there was nothing we could do. In a town of so many thousands there were bound to be a few unfortunate and hopeless, and we couldn't stop them from jumping. We couldn't make them want to live, nor could we change the currents that washed them to a certain place on a certain shore every time they jumped. This became an issue every few years, a point of contention between those of us on the mainland and those on the islands to our west. Nothing was ever done. A law was passed forbidding lovers from kissing on the precipice, but I believe that was all. And while the rest of us huddled alone in our dark rooms, my father always read very late into the night.

A NIGHT LIKE THIS

I was with a woman the other night, the first time I'd been with one in a while. I'm not going to give her a name here because I'm not sure her name is all that important: for the sake of this story, she could have been anybody. That sounds mean, but it's true. She could have been any number of women, I think, even though things had worked out with us well enough to the point that we were together, we seemed to like each other, and we were all set to take that next step. We'd gone through the preliminaries: the dinners, the movies, sharing highlights from our pasts like movie trailers, and then the gradual physical intimacy that began with a brief kiss on the first date and then a deep one on the second and a very complicated and tangled maneuver on her couch on the third, which left us both breathless, wanting more. But we were pacing ourselves, just being together a little bit before the inevitable happened. Because both of us knew that the next time we saw each other we'd sleep together. It's not something we said outright, but we both knew it was going to happen.

I thought about it all week. I must have thought about it ten times a day, imagining this woman with her clothes off, or me taking them off, and then me with *my* clothes off, on top of her, you know, or wherever, wondering how it would all play out. When you're married for a while you trade in that mystery for comfort, and while the excitement level can be low there's nothing like being with a friend, making love with someone who doesn't care if you look a certain way, different from Brad Pitt or whoever, and who accepts you as you are, who actually *wants* you as you are. That's the way it is in a good marriage, folks, at least that's the way it was in mine. But it's not like I ever thought about making love to my wife ten times a day. We just did it. Then, usually, we'd go to sleep. I shouldn't keep calling her my wife. But it's hard to rename somebody after calling them one thing for so long. It's a lot to ask, to start calling her my *ex*-wife, just like that. It's only been a few months. I'm trying but I'm not there yet. It's like having a new telephone number, or the first few weeks after the year changes. It takes time to get it right.

So anyway, finally the night came. This woman and I had a little dinner at the new Mexican place, which was good. A couple of margaritas apiece. She was funny, and clever, and we were both laughing. I loved her laugh. Things went well.

Back at my place, my apartment, events proceeded rapidly. I mean the door was barely closed before we were all over each other, kissing right there in the hallway, our bodies close. It had been six months since anything like this had happened, and I couldn't believe I had gone so long without it. I don't know how long it had been for her, I never asked, but I could tell we were on the same page. It was heated and beautiful at the same time. The way it's supposed to feel when two people like each other, and might, who knows, fall in love.

No reason to go into every detail, though. You know what happens. This isn't a how-to manual. By the time we made it into my bed we were naked, except that she was wearing her socks and I had my watch on. A couple of times I nicked her with it and apologized. And though I'd been worried that I wasn't going to be able to perform, it having been so long and this woman being the first since being with the same woman for twelve years, I did pretty well, I think, all things considered, and I think that she was happy too, though I felt I shouldn't ask. I don't know what to do anymore, how to be. But it was probably a good idea not to ask.

After it was over, we lay beside each other, breathing. As fast paced as everything had been up until then, it was weird, just lying there, still. I'd left the bathroom light on, with the door cracked, and a thin path of light edged across the room and fell against my dresser. We were both looking at it. On the top of the dresser was a little photograph of my wife, unframed; it was leaning against the bare wall, the only picture in the whole room. I missed her, there was no getting around that. I missed her body. I missed watching her take her shirt off, the way she crossed her arms in an *X*, taking the hem of the shirt in her fingers and pulling it upward over her head, exposing her bra and then her breasts, drooping like teardrops, soft as rain. I missed the sentences she never finished, the words she never found. I missed the *idea* of her as my wife, to have and to hold. I missed her saying, "Well I'll be." And when because some friend of hers was brokenhearted and out of anger and empathy she condemned the men of the world wholesale as terrible, inhumane creatures, she always looked at me and smiled and said, "Present company excluded." I liked that, and I missed that, and I wished I had a chance to hear her say it again. I had found the picture the other day and something about it, I don't know, it was just a nice shot of her. But looking at it now, with this woman, it made me wish I had put it away.

"Who's that?" she asked me.

"That picture?" I said. "Nobody."

"Well," she said, with a little laugh. "It's *somebody*."

"You know what I mean," I said.

"Is that, like, your girlfriend?"

"No," I said. "I don't have a girlfriend."

But maybe I shouldn't have said it like that, because if I had a girlfriend it was her. I could tell this stung her. The air in the room changed then, and she seemed to move away from me a little on the bed. Our arms had been touching but they weren't anymore, and her face, when I looked at it, had lost something. A friendliness.

"Is it your wife?" she asked me.

"No," I said. "No. I mean, it is, she was, but she's not anymore. I told you that."

"And you have her picture on your dresser?"

"It's just a picture," I said. "One picture."

And I thought how true that was, how it was only a picture, a moment a picture had fixed in time, one moment out of all of them. It was just her standing there, doing nothing special, at a time before when she was my wife. And here I was looking at it with this new woman.

"It's none of my business," she said, "but I should tell you, you know, for the next time this happens to you. It's maybe best not to have a picture of your ex-wife on display. It kills the mood."

She smiled at me then, in a friendly way, and I knew, just the way I knew a week ago we were going to be having sex that night, that we were never going to be having it again. It just wasn't going to work out. I knew we weren't going to be seeing each other, all because of that picture I had on my dresser and the way the light fell on it so that we both could see. The way she said *the next time this happens to you.* The next woman, she meant. The next her. And I thought, How wonderful. How wonderful that I would get to go through this all again, the movies and dinners, the incremental kissing, the flirting, the figuring each other out, the getting to like each other, just to get right back to this same place, the beginning of something good. Christ, I thought, I might have to do it for the rest of my life. Who could say? Not me: I'd be the last person to know. I'd be the last person in the whole world. And all of a sudden I was glad I had that picture of my wife up there now, illuminated in the light, so we could all see whose fault this was. I hated her, hated her so much in that moment. But it passed.

"She's pretty," the woman said. "Your ex-wife."

"Well, she takes a good picture," I said.

And that was that. I took the woman home, the two of us sharing that terrible quiet, and watched her walk the long walk that led to her door. Then I drove away, and for some reason started laughing. Because it struck me as funny, I think, how fucked up we can be and still manage to carry on. Not *we* really, but me: *I* was fucked up, and here I was carrying on—like a soldier, or a dark and quiet hero, and that was kind of funny. It was a cool night, a starry sky, and I drove without a thought of where I was going, through the dark parts of town, the lights of the city glowing in the distance. The wind slipped in through my window and was soft against my skin. It felt good. The wind felt good. It was like feeling like you're in a movie, that your life is a movie and this is one of the good parts, where the sweet music starts to play. I could even see a piece of the moon, shy tonight, but full behind a glowing bank of clouds. Perfect. It would be a night like this, I hoped, when I would suddenly realize I wasn't married anymore, like the day you get the year right, or remember your telephone number without thinking about it, or when you can tell somebody where you live, the new place, and call it home, and mean it.

NEIGHBOR

I remember the old man perched in his second-story window, milky behind the wavy glass, glaring at all us kids like we were the mice and he was the hungry hawk. We played in his yard sometimes. I never met him. I thought—in my nightmares—that one day he'd pitch himself through the window and grab one of us, hold us in his arms until we crumbled, sucking our life out through his withered, chicken-skinned body and dragging himself back inside, appearing at the window again, waiting for another one of us to drift into his gaze, living forever. He didn't live, though: one day he died. It happened the way it happens when you're young: on a different plane, like clouds. I just remember wearing the coat and tie I never wore, and the shoes so tight my toes bled, in a church we never went to, surrounded by the smell of the strange and the old. We went back to his house after, and I went inside for the first time. His ancient wife shivered in a big green chair on an Oriental rug, not even crying. I think she was all dried up. I ate a little sandwich, then I went outside to see if he was still there at the window—and he was. I knew he would be. He waved, all friendly now, and I waved back, I don't know why. My throat felt strangled, my eyes so dry I thought they'd crack. Then he disappeared, fading back into the dark, and I never saw him there again. I didn't tell anybody. How could I? I didn't know what it meant, or what it could mean, because even though I was young I knew I didn't believe in anything. I told my wife about it, though, twenty years later. We were in bed in the dark. Just married, our lives ahead of us—so far ahead we couldn't even see them from where we were. I wanted to tell her everything, though, everything about me, and so I did, and part of the everything was this. It had stayed with me all these years. The story scared her, of course, but not the way it had scared me. I asked her what she thought it meant. *It means you'll be a ghost one day*, she said, *and so will I*, and she cried as if this were the first time it had ever occurred to her, because she never wanted to think that even this—all of this, our brand-new world together, the love so big we almost couldn't bear it—wasn't going to last. *It means I won't be with you forever*, she said. And she was right.

THE LONG ROAD HOME IS
COVERED IN LIMPID ROSES

My father—old, alone, penniless, six or seven warrants out for his arrest—came to stay with me for what turned out to be the rest of his life. He'd lived under a dozen aliases in his seventy-one years, but his real name was the one people thought he'd made up: Teddy Sandwich. "Like the Earl," he was fond of saying, right before he stole your watch. He hadn't changed much since the last time I saw him a decade ago: worn and grizzled as an interstate-exit hobo, shoes that looked like socks, and a twitch he'd had since licking an electrical outlet on a bet.

He flopped on the couch, lit a cigarette after I asked him not to, and apologized.

"I'm sorry, kid," he said. "You really don't deserve this, and by this of course I mean me." And what could I say? He was right. I'd lived a good life. I was a middle-school science teacher, track coach, advisor to the school paper, *The Plucky Lion*. I didn't date much because no woman could live up to my impossibly high standards. I was lonely in a virtuous way.

Then he narrowed his eyes. "But I guess this is what you get for killing your twin."

"Killing my—? Dad, please. Jesus." He made this kind of shit up all the time, just to put you back on your heels. "What a terrible thing to say."

"In the womb," he said. "You killed him in the womb."

"For God's sake. Enough."

He shrugged. "Whatever. Bottom line is, you're all I got." And then, under his breath: "Murderer."

My father was the worst, frankly, maybe even the worst of the worst. I knew him some because my mother made me stay with him a couple of summers while she pursued a modeling career in Japan. She was on billboards for Suntory whiskey from Nagoya to Niigata. I hated every minute of being with him. My whole life since then I'd ask myself, "What would my father do?" and then I'd do exactly the opposite. Sporting his vices like a new silk jacket, he bilked old ladies out of minor fortunes, sold nonexistent beachfront real estate, and smoked like a California wildfire, like he got paid per cigarette: one always hung from the side of his mouth like a malignant appendage, or smoldered on a dinner plate, on the television set—whatever was handy. As if water were too rare and precious a commodity to be used for mere vanity, he rarely bathed. He slept whenever he had a notion to: sometimes from noon to four, or three in the morning to five, up before dawn. And he sleepwalked, wandering around the house muttering words he'd never use awake.

Subterfuge. Elegant fornicators. The long road home is covered in limpid roses. He had a scary charm. My mother said people gave him money just so he wouldn't wreck their lives, which he could do with a phone call. You could tell this was something he would be good at. He brought home stray dogs, one a week or so, and some dogs who were not strays at all, dogs whose collars he'd remove and toss into the gutter. He loved dogs more than me and he'd be the first to admit it.

I was once bitten by a vicious basset hound he nicked from a schoolyard and my father rushed to its aid lickety-split.

"Are you okay, buddy boy?"

"It bit *me*, Dad," I said as I bandaged my hand with a sock I found under the coffee table. "I was just going to pet him."

"I wondered what it was you did," he hissed. "And don't look at me that way." He rubbed the basset's head with a tenderness I never once experienced. "If it's a crime to love dogs then lock me up!"

He was locked up on several occasions but not for loving dogs.

His penis (those words perhaps the most difficult I have ever written) was big, bigger than mine by a lot, something I wish I didn't know but something that, clearly, he wanted me to, the way he Donald-Ducked it around the house until he had his first cup of coffee.

He talked shit about my mother. They'd been married

for less than a year when she left him, and he never failed to stick a knife in her memory.

"She asked for a lot, your mom," he liked to say. "She wanted to eat my soul!"

Always up to something, Dad was. One day he took a folding chair to the end of the driveway, wearing light blue boxers and an undershirt and a top hat from his circus days, and told the fortunes of everyone who passed, whether they wanted one told or not.

"Hey, lady! You're going to find love in the strangest of places. Like a parking lot or a public restroom." To a man in a nice suit: "You, my friend, are going to lose your hair—in a horrific way." And to a dog, walking on a leather leash by the old lady who gave apples for treats on Halloween: "You're going to be rich one day, my friend. Your owner has more money than sin and not a friend in the world. She's leaving it all to you."

He once let his head fall face-first into a bowl of spaghetti and tomato sauce and he stayed that way for over a minute. That's a long time to have your face in a bowl of spaghetti.

All I have are stories like this about my father, this guy who woke up every morning of his life wondering if he was dead and, discovering he wasn't, just did whatever the fuck he wanted to, because why not? He was alive and life was a thing to be lived, not pussied around with, not wasted following rules you don't know who invented them and what their angle was in the making of. "If I teach you any god damn thing," he said to me one day, "the god damn thing I would teach you is not to learn any god damn thing. It's all just mind control, in one form or another."

"The same way exercise is body control," I said, exercise being another thing he didn't believe in. He was skinny as a stick. I couldn't see a muscle anywhere on his body, just skin and ribs, a pathetic, flaccid meat sack.

There were no rules in his world, no certainties, not even taxes (which he never paid), just the one thing, death. But that wasn't happening to him either, because here he was in my guest room, lively as hell.

"How did you find me?" I said. "Mom wouldn't tell you."

"Internet at the library. You're the only Theodore Sandwich Jr. in existence, believe it or not." He tried to light a cigarette, but the match died due to his violently shaking hand. Took him three tries. "Parkinson's," he said. "A couple of years and I'll be as wooden as a cigar store Indian."

"Native American," I said. "A cigar store Native American."

Long story short: he was right. Eventually he just froze up. Two years later all he could do was blink. A year later he died from ossification of the heart. My mother came all the way from Atlanta to see him at the morgue, just to make sure he was dead. (He'd often pretended to die, mostly to escape the Feds.)

Mother and I went out to dinner after and celebrated. She was a retired billboard model by then. Still beautiful, just the older kind. We talked about what a terrible man my father was, and how neither of us were sorry that he was dead, not in the least. After living with him for three years and doing everything I had to do for him, my heart had ossified too.

I paid for dinner and I walked her to her car. Then I asked her something that had been on my mind for a long, long time.

"So, Mom, weird question. Did I—did I have a twin? In the womb I mean? Dad said."

She gave me a poisonous look.

"He told you that. I can't believe he told you that."

"I know. He said I had a twin and that I 'killed him in the womb.' It's ridiculous. And just like him to say something like that, right?"

I sort of laughed to get her to look at me. But she wouldn't.

"Well, thing is, you *did* kill him," she said. "I never wanted you to know and made him promise not to tell you. But you did it. We could see it happening on the ultrasound. The stealthy approach from behind, your little hands around his little neck. The doctor said you were the strongest fetus he had ever seen, that your brother never had a chance. He was smaller than you were, you know, the sensitive one. Really sad and awful."

"I did that? Oh my God, that's terrible."

"Your father thought it was hilarious, of course."

"Hilarious?"

"Yeah. He always said, 'One little Sandwich is enough.' When we'd go out to lunch, he'd always make the same joke, saying he was thinking about getting a big sandwich, but then he would say, 'But maybe one little sandwich is enough,' and laugh. He was always making jokes about the brother you killed in the womb and that's really why I left him." She had her hand on the door handle, her eyes focused on nothing, just thinking, as if she were reviewing the years between then and now. She shrugged, and looked at me, I thought, with a mixture of love and pity. It was the way she had looked at me all my life. Now I knew why. "All things considered you turned out better than I thought you would. Much better."

She may have said something else but my head was all static by then. She kissed me on the cheek and drove away. The Miata backfired as she rounded the corner and disappeared, and somehow I knew I'd never see her again. Spoiler alert: I didn't.

The restaurant was just a few blocks from my place, so I walked home. I was in a daze, felt like she'd bricked me across the temple, so I went the long way, through the nicer neighborhoods, and I took it slow. I had a lot to think about. I was a murderer now, after all. I'd always been one, I guess, but knowing it changed things. It changed everything. I felt like me, but different—a different me. Like me, in many ways identical to me, but being taken over by something strange and foreign.

Night had fallen. Light spilled from the windows of the fancy brownstones. Beyond the windows, mothers were putting their children to bed, fathers were putting the dishes away. Happy fucking families. I kind of watched myself watching them—as if I were hovering in the air above me, looking down. And looking down at me I saw who I was, just this guy, this lonely nobody with nothing, *this murderer*, walking down the sidewalk, alone.

I'd never been so low, not in all of my years on this planet.

And then I stopped in my tracks. Because something came to me, a revelation like the holy men have. And it was this: I was free. There was nothing I couldn't do now. Nothing. I had already done the worst thing a person could do, and so whatever I did from here on out, no matter how bad it was, how crazy, how stupid, how pointless and selfish and destructive, would pale in comparison. I was free, and true freedom is like a superpower. I know that now. It's like being invisible. No one could see me, but oh, I could see myself. I knew who I was. I followed my fate like it was a siren, and from that day forward I lived and lived and lived, and I watched the incidental damage my life produced pile up in the rearview mirror. I was a Sandwich, after all—Theodore Sandwich Jr., the only one in the world.

GONE

She waited almost two days before calling the police. Even though she knew in the pit of her stomach that something was terribly wrong—her husband had never gone a single day without talking to her, much less two, not in fifteen years of marriage—calling the police still felt a little dramatic, even clichéd. She'd spoken to his mother and father, his kid sister, the friend he played handball with, and his poker buddies, his assistant at work, neighbors (could they have seen anything?), cryptically fishing for information as to where he might be and got nothing. She had to call. But as soon as she dialed those numbers—9-1-1—she felt not like a wife whose husband had disappeared but a character in a television show, a woman playing the part of a wife whose husband has disappeared.

An operator at the police station answered and said exactly what they always said on the TV shows.

"911, what is the exact address of your emergency?"

"208 Ridgecrest Drive," she said.

"What's your emergency?"

Amy felt challenged, as if she had better have a good

emergency or she'd somehow fail this test. "I'd like to re-port—not to report, I mean, I don't know, but I think some-thing may have happened to my husband. Something."

The operator was a woman. She was silent as Amy thrashed her way through the sentence. Had Amy actually seen a television show once where the woman said exactly that, had stuttered in exactly that way? Possibly. Amy loved crime dramas. She loved the fragile, temporary terror and the reassurance that all would be well at the end of an hour, just in time for dinner.

"What makes you think something has happened to your husband?" the operator said. "Tell me exactly what hap-pened." She sounded sober and bureaucratic and humorless. She sounded like she was taking notes. *8:19 p.m. Received call from woman claiming something may have happened to her husband. Shaky voice. Very nervous. Suspicious.*

"What makes me think something has—? Two days. I haven't heard from him in two days."

"Okay. Go on."

"I don't—that doesn't happen. He's never—even a day—"

She wished she'd stop stuttering because she sounded like an idiot. She wasn't an idiot: she was a professor of me-dieval literature at a private university. But somehow here, in the twenty-first century, on the telephone to someone prob-ably half her age, she was fumbling over every word. Her emotions curled around her brain and choked it.

"When was the last time you saw him?"

She saw his jacket, his back, late for work, the door rushing to close behind him, the words *I love you* cut off by its slam, but she thought that's what he said because that's what he always said. *I love you*, he said, probably, not *I'm leaving you.*

"On his way to work," she said.

"And?"

"He went to work, then he left work early at the end of the day."

"You're sure?"

"I think I'm sure. That's what they told me."

"And you have some reason to believe they weren't telling you the truth?"

"No. No reason."

"Then you're sure."

"Yes, I'm sure."

The woman on the other end sighed. *Like pulling teeth, getting this one to say the simplest things. Like there was something she was trying not to say. Something she was hiding.*

"Are there any places to your knowledge where he might have gone? A cabin? His parents' home? A motel room?"

"A *motel* room?"

The operator breathed into the receiver. In the background Amy could hear other operators just like this one doing the same thing. Finding lost husbands. "I don't know what you mean, a motel room."

"It's just a place to go, ma'am, when people don't want to be found."

"Why wouldn't he want to be found?"

"Ma'am," she said again, more forcefully, but also tired, frustrated. Amy hated that word: *ma'am.* "I'm just asking you questions to try to determine the nature of your situation. But we can't even open a file until three days have passed. You'll need to call back tomorrow."

This was *insane.* "Then why have we even been having this conversation?"

"I'm just trying to *help,*" the operator said. "Sometimes just talking about it makes you remember something, something that happened, something special, a clue, the way he was, how he was with you the last time you saw him, something you said, didn't say, something *he* said, maybe about a place, a new friend, the distance between you, the way it grows and grows and sometimes you can't tell it's there until there's such a gulf that it's impossible to even find the person, where he's gone, where he went, and what you did to make that happen."

"What *I* did?"

"Ma'am. For all I know you may have killed him and this is the beginning of a ruse to deceive us. He may be in the garden, cut up in a dozen shoebox-size pieces."

"Oh my God. I would never—"

"Of course not. But if you had, you would say the exact same thing. I'm just trying to help. Covering all the bases."

"Of course," Amy said. "Thank you. Thank you for trying to help."

Silence. Then the operator said, "Well?"

"Well what?"

"Does anything come to you? Anything you did? Anything at all?"

But nothing did. It was as if she had been drained of every thought and emotion, that she was just this husk, nothing, not *real*. As if she were playing the part of a wife whose husband had disappeared, and she didn't know her next line, what the rest of the story was, what she was supposed to say now, how this was all going to be resolved. And so she waited for someone—the director, the writer, her own heart, whoever or whatever had gotten Amy into this—to tell her what it was.

HOW TO BUILD A COFFIN

Building a coffin is a demanding but satisfying project for the ambitious carpenter to undertake, and entails a number of skills, including edging, corner joinery, trim, and finishing. You don't have to be an expert carpenter, but the more experience you have the stronger the coffin will be. The last thing you want is for your coffin to fall apart. Ninety-four pounds may not seem like a lot, but if the corner joinery is weak you can bet on disaster. You can bet on catastrophe. *Better safe than sorry*, as my wife would say.

Choosing the wood. Hardwood-veneered plywood is made of thin slices of hardwood, including oak, birch, maple, ash, or cherry, that are factory glued to a soft, plywood substrate. You can buy this at any lumber store. Depending on the time of year it may have to be special ordered, so it's a good idea to start the process a week or two before you're actually going to need it. You may find this difficult; building a coffin while its future occupant is still alive presents a number of questions, among them being, *You're not God, how do you know for sure she's going to die?* Well, just look at her. She weighs ninety-four pounds! You think she's going to live? You hope so, sure, but hope was something you gave up last month, so the most productive thing you can do now is build a coffin. It's a good—and practical—distraction. Just hope she doesn't hear you hammering.

Corner joinery. I know: I'm a broken record when it comes to corner joinery, but it's by far the most important part of this project. You can use fluted dowels or plug-covered screws. Screws are especially attractive for three reasons: they don't demand special equipment, they act as their own clamps by drawing the sides and ends together, and they are ideal for caskets destined to be shipped long distances, if, for instance, the future occupant insists on being buried in a plot in California, beside her mother and father, even if she moved to North Carolina years before, following her husband, who could find work nowhere else. One thing to take into consideration here is if this decision, this *desire* to be buried so far, far away, was made under duress, or if her mind was muddled by medication, or maybe the chemo. In those instances, it should fall to the husband to decide, regardless of what other family members might think. But just in case, use the screws.

Trim and finishing. Moldings make an enormous difference to the look of any do-it-yourself casket. As a general rule, put the largest moldings along the bottom, smaller moldings around the lid. Personalizing your coffin, of course, is one big advantage of the handmade option. Create a design. Carve her initials on the side. You can add custom cushions to the interior, or maybe just wrap a favorite quilt around some bed pillows. Are you really going to keep those pillows anyway? They're covered in hair, her hair, hair as brown as it was the day you met her. What kind of life would that be? Especially if you fulfill her last request, which is to remarry. The new wife can't be expected to sleep with that quilt, those pillows, in that bed—not that you have plans to remarry, but who knows, things might change. Things *will* change. That's the thing about things: change is all they do.

Summary. That about covers it. Following these instructions will ensure your coffin will be the best possible coffin you could build, a box you can be proud of—or a box of which you can be proud, for those of you, like her, whose goal in life it was never to end a sentence with a preposition. I don't mean that. She had other goals, many, among them: to be kind, to love me with all my heart, to live a longer life. But what can you do? Nothing, it turns out. You can't do anything, so you might as well build her a coffin. In a way it's like holding her forever—like that, but *not* that. Nothing is like that. Nothing, nothing, nothing.

THE BIG CURVE

The last time I saw my dad he was wearing a toupee that looked like a year's worth of dryer lint, a Dallas Cowboys T-shirt, green golfing shorts, and penny loafers with actual pennies in them. No socks. He was waving at my wife and me as we drove away in the car he had just given us; he said he wouldn't be needing it anymore. I watched him in the rearview mirror down the long driveway and into the street, until he stopped waving, his arm slowly dropping to his side, and then watched him watch us as we disappeared around the Big Curve, the hairpin, where who knows how many lives had been lost—*lost* we called them, as if they might be found again one day. I told my wife, *When I was kid we weren't allowed beyond the Big Curve on our bikes; he thought it was just too dangerous. Always had to turn around when we got here, go back home.*

He watched us go. He waited for our return.

CASSIE

I thought it might be a dead body. I don't know why, something about the thump of it: solid, heavy—and then—nothing. A silence like death, right outside my bedroom window. I was asleep when I heard it and woke as if shaken, the way my husband used to do, gently, by the shoulder. The wind blew hard that night, and my neighbors—who so often left their porch light on hours after they should have—had turned it off. Usually they left it on for their daughter; she didn't come home before midnight on the weekends, if then, out with the boys from her school, I'm sure, and the girls, who drank and who knows what else—smoking whatever it is they smoke now—and, I mean, why not? I'm not against it, really, whatever it was they did. She was seventeen years old. I can only imagine the things she got herself into, and I probably would have done the same had I been her, had I been a girl now instead of when I was one: trouble wasn't as easy to come by then. Cassandra—the neighbor's daughter, that was her name. But they called her Cassie. The light was for her, so even when everything else was dark—no moon, no stars—she would know where to go. She wouldn't trip or fall into a ditch or wander over to my house, thinking my home was hers, something comically sad like that. A drunk teenager, wandering over here and pounding at the door screaming *Mother!* until I opened up and she saw it was me, old Mrs. Murphy, the nosey next-door neighbor who walks to the mailbox everyday wearing her slippers—her *slippers*—sometimes waiting at the mailbox for it, holding up the mailman for a good five minutes before letting him get back to work, like she has no one else in the world to talk to.

It was a yellow bulb, always on. A yellow bulb was supposed to discourage the insects from swarming, but I don't think those bulbs really work that well. It was *very* yellow, though. Even the shadows turned yellow as they fell through my window and onto the walls and ceiling of my bedroom, and if I'd yet to fully draw the curtains and shut the shades the light fell right into my eyes. *I won't complain*, I told myself again and again, by which I meant I won't be the woman who complains, who calls them on the telephone during dinner or leaves the note in the mailbox. I didn't even want to be the woman who *wants* to say something, who *wishes* she could say something to them, about the light, about their daughter, about what she does at night, but won't because she doesn't want to be known as that kind of woman and yet, even so, becomes her all the same.

But there was no light for Cassie tonight. The dark kept me up for hours that night. At some point I went to sleep, though, and that's when I heard it: the terrible sound of the body as it fell to the ground outside my bedroom window, her body, this girl I'd watched become a woman before my very eyes, from whom my Girl Scout cookies were religiously bought, and who became beautiful, with a big laugh, lovely blonde hair, and sweet blue eyes. I knew what had happened, could see it without looking: she was sprawled beneath my shrubs, her arms and legs unnaturally splayed, eyes swelled shut by the bruises, her blouse ripped and bloodied. And I could see the years ahead, living beside her parents and their childless home, watching them wonder what it was they did or didn't do, what they could have done differently to change what could no longer be changed. Should they have insisted she work harder in school? Make her bed? Stay away from those boys? Get a job? Knowing that anything they might or might not have done could have changed everything. You know, something as simple as sending her on an errand, a trip to the store to get some milk for her family, even that— who knows?—may have changed her world such that she would have stayed home that evening, or gone to a movie with a different boy, or somehow thought better of what she did not end up thinking better about. That's life, though, and that's how her mother and father would spend the rest of theirs, thinking about how it might have been different, dried and hollow husks of people not even really alive anymore themselves. This is who the world will cry for.

But what about me? What about me, I thought, in my bedroom that night, in my queen-size bed, alone. *What about me?* I'm the one who heard her fall. It was under my window she bled and died. Not once did I ask the neighbors to turn out their light—not once! And yet they did, they did, and I could have told them, this is what happens when you do.

Two police cars came, then a fire truck, and an ambulance. Blue lights, red lights, white lights—it was like Christmas. They were here for some time. But the officers couldn't find anything suspicious—nothing—and told me the noise likely came from the wind, the wind that had blown so hard that night I woke as if snatched back into the world by an unseen hand.

DRUNK, I KISSED HER

Drunk, I kissed her, and drunk, she kissed me. I remember her tongue barreling into my mouth as if it were looking for another place to live, and we were holding onto each other so hard, like fighters against the ropes. It started late that night on the couch beside the bookcase in Spencer's parents' house, the last party before we left for college. I'd never kept my eyes closed for so long still awake and with all my clothes on, and even though I couldn't see anything I knew her eyes were closed too, because she was feeling every part of me as if she were blind and were trying to understand who this was she was attached to now, who was attached to her. We opened our eyes at the same time, and when I lifted my face from hers I discovered that the party was over, all of our friends were gone. We could see where they'd been: the mostly empty bottles of wine, beer cans crushed and scattered across the cracked glass coffee table, an ashtray full of dead soldiers, though some were still alive, barely smoldering. I realized we'd been on top of each other, lips locked on this ratty couch in front of everyone, so shut away in our own world we didn't care and had chased them all away.

"Where are we?" she said. "Spencer's?"

"Yeah, Spencer's."

She looked a little dizzy.

"This is *crazy*," she said, brushing strands of her hair from my mouth. But she didn't let go and neither did I. I licked her salty neck and she closed her eyes again, and this time I watched her, and she looked like someone I had made up: so pretty in a lopsided kind of way, sort of smiling, but sad. She looked like someone I would never see again. We held hands and stood up together, leaning against each other, swaying. I could see somebody's feet on a bed through a half-open door to the bedroom.

We left. Even walking down two flights of stairs I didn't let go of her and we stopped halfway down to kiss again for a minute or two, my right thumb slipped into a loop of her jeans.

Outside it was so dark, the sky filled with dull pieces of golden glitter.

"Where are we going?" she said.

"My house. It's not far. My mom's home, though. We'll just have to be quiet."

My mother wouldn't care, I thought, or maybe she would, but I just couldn't summon the will to figure out which it might be.

The night air was soft. I remember that.

"Where are you going next year?"

It's what I asked everybody that summer, and what everybody asked me. But I hadn't asked her yet.

"State," she said. "You?"

"Same," I said.

She took my hand and squeezed. But it turned out her State and my State were in different states. And we kept walking into the dark, finally stumbling over the curb of a traffic island and falling into the grass. I swear I never held anyone closer than I held her then, this woman I had just met, only hours ago. That seemed impossible now. But I've never understood how time works.

A car drove by. A couple was inside it. I caught a picture of them briefly, an old man driving and an old woman sitting next to him. The headlights spotlighted us like movie stars for about three seconds, but the car didn't stop and we watched its red taillights disappear around the bend. I wondered if they had seen us, clutching each other on the shore of this island.

She brought her lips to my ear and whispered. "I can barely breathe!" she said, and then laughed with a small but perfect joy.

I let her go a little, then a lot.

FOREVER

Since Marianne was leaving this town forever, what did it matter what she did now? If she walked down Third Street naked, or failed to recycle, or ordered a big meal, ate it, and left without paying? Or told all of the boys who'd done wrong by her (two) why her story would end quite happily and chances were theirs would not? None of these things did she do (wasn't her style), but it wouldn't have mattered if she did. Nothing mattered anymore because this town had ceased to exist to her. It was not a place on the planet: she was just the only one who knew that. Everyone else here went on living as if there were a point to themselves. And that's the joke, she thought, on them.

She could be halfway to California by this time tomorrow.

But moving was hard. Packing was hard. One has so much stuff. She couldn't take *everything*. She didn't want to take everything. She just wanted enough to get to the next place, where stuff would be new, and if not new (which, face it, it wouldn't be, it would be years before she had anything even remotely new) at least different. The last thing she wanted to do was take so much with her that she was making her new life out of the things her old life was made of. Birds make new nests every year out of new twigs—they don't use the old twigs: those were last year's nest.

But she had to take a few of the old twigs because she wasn't a bird. She was seventeen years old and leaving home with great dispatch. Socks and shoes and some nice shirts, her three favorite T-shirts. A ring she had and a spangled bracelet and two necklaces, one just a teardrop sapphire on a silver chain and the other a gold cross, because that seemed to say so much about her without her having to say anything. It said, *I'm a good girl.* She hadn't been that good so far and she wasn't sure how good she was going to be in the future. But it was always a good idea to have a cross.

People called this *running away* but she thought that wasn't really it: it was *running toward.* At seventeen, she was just a little early. It was leaving something bad and finding something good. Sure, her father was a drunk and he'd popped her once, hard so she wouldn't forget, so that all the other times all he had to do was raise his hand, but even that felt like a swat. Her mother took a hunky-dory approach, pretending it didn't happen or that it wasn't all that bad, really, *grow up Marianne, for God's sake it could be so much worse,* and that too was a hurt. It just wasn't working out for her anymore so off she was going.

She thought about writing a note but wanted to get a ways away before they alerted the law to come looking for her: buses are turtle slow. She'd call from a pay phone and let them know she was alive, and okay, that she was better than okay, she was *fantastic*, walking on her own yellow brick road for some time by then.

So, Mom at work, Dad looking for work, she stuffed her stuff into an army-green satchel and headed out. As she opened the front door she heard a cry—Rusty, her old calico. Rusty cat-walked briskly over to her legs, where she leaned against them and somehow without stopping performed her signature figure eight around them. All that furry, purring warmth. Marianne set down her bag, sat on the floor, and rubbed the cat's head. Then Marianne licked her fingers and did what she thought Rusty's cat mother might have done, rubbing her ears and the brown half circles beneath her eyes. Blue-eyed Rusty, pound cat eight years ago, her biography being that she along with a passel of brothers and sisters were left in a box on the side of State Road 15, rescued, and—happy ending—all had found good homes. Rusty was the last of the litter picked. She was cross-eyed and her tail looked a little short. Marianne would miss her. She didn't worry about Rusty, though. Cats might be smart, but they did not have the brains to understand how things worked. All a cat knows is that you were there or you weren't there, and who knows how long it had been since either thing happened. When Marianne walked out that door Rusty wouldn't know and she never would. All she would know is that one minute Marianne was here, the next not.

And then that next minute came and she *was* gone, closing the door behind her with a solid click of the lock, and Rusty sat there for a moment, taking it all in, and then meandered into the living room hoping to resume the sleep she had been working on earlier. But she changed her mind, and instead of reclaiming her spot on the silky green sofa, she took the stairs and headed into Marianne's room, where she settled on Marianne's bed, right in the middle, paws tucked beneath her, and waited, forever.

SNOW

The last time I saw my mother she was digging through the snow after my little brother, who had disappeared into a drift. This happened a lot—brother disappearing into the snow—but there was nothing we could do; Samuel was a fast one, and if you tried to catch him he'd laugh in your face and before you knew it he'd lose you in the brambles or the moss or, in this case, it being winter, the snow. People said it drove Mom half crazy, but the truth is it drove her crazy all the way. Like this: for the last year or so she'd been shooting at squirrels with a straw and a handful of dried chickpeas. She was a pretty good shot, too: she blinded one of them. But her dream of a stew in which there was a squirrel never materialized. She thought of little else all day long, and on that day as well—*squirrels, squirrels, squirrels*—until Samuel disappeared into the snow and she had to find him. He was but seven years old to my seventeen. *Come help me find your brother*, she'd call to me, but I'd learned my lesson; I wasn't going to give him the pleasure. I'd be out there up to my jaw in snow and he'd call to us from the fiery warmth of the house, waving and cackling like the imp he was. *Forget about him!* I called out to her. *He'll be back.* But she could never forget about little Samuel, who was named after our good-for-nothing, horse-thieving father, the devil take him. My mother dug and I watched from the porch, blowing on my hands to keep off the frost.

Then it was all, *Samuel! I see you, you little scamp!* And into the snow she dove.

And all was silence. The winter world allowed not a sound. *Mom?* I said, cautious at first. Didn't want to get overwrought unless it was called for. *Mom? Mom?* And I stood and I looked out at the beautiful white snow blanket that had only moments before been like the ocean and its waves, and they were the things Mom was diving into and now all it was was a white shroud of cold. I ran out into the awful snow, running, almost jumping because as soft as it was, running through it was like running in a dream. Where was Mom? Where was Samuel? I had seen where she was last, but by the time I got to where I thought it was, that place had been all covered over by falling snow, and so I wasn't sure whether this was the spot or not, because it was all a field of white, and it all seemed to go on and on forever.

Of course, that's when I heard him. *Hey!* he said. He was on the porch, all wrapped up in his favorite blankie. *Tell Mom I'm home and warming my feet by the fire.* And he cackled a bit, the way he did.

The sun was going down. Soon night would fall and it would all be as black as it was white right now. I didn't know what to do. I kicked around, hoping I might somehow discover her, half frozen, and save her life. But I didn't. I never saw her again, even after the snow thawed the next spring. It happened so fast: there was this moment when we had a mom, and then there was the next, when we didn't. I was on my way out of there too, gone from that crappy shack, gone from our crappy town, tomorrow maybe, maybe the next. I saw there was a life for me out in the bright world. But that all changed; that life was gone. There was no *next* for me anymore, without Mom. It was just me and Samuel now, forever. That's what I was thinking as Mom was out there somewhere freezing in the snow: *poor me.* All I thought of was myself while my mom was turning to ice, and that's when I knew I was the worst, the worst of us all, of anybody, the very worst.

So I scraped the snow off of my pants and my shoes and I went inside. Samuel was there all happy and warm and grinning ear to ear, having fooled her good this time.

I'm hungry, he said. *When's dinner?*

Soon. And I picked up the straw, a handful of chickpeas. *Soon.*

LAURA, LINDA, SWEETIE PIE

She went crazy, briefly, in the fall, and tried to kill him. He wrote a story about it. In the story her name was Maureen, and instead of putting little pieces of gravel in the chocolate cake she was making for him, he had her put little pieces of gravel—and glass—in a strawberry tart. Nice touch, he thought, the glass. *Glinting in the bright kitchen light.*

She recovered just as the story was appearing in a magazine, and she read it, and sued him. He wrote about that too, finishing a short piece before the trial itself was over. In that story he wasn't an author and she wasn't formerly crazy, but everything else was just about the same. In the writing he was somehow able to eke out a happy ending, with her actually dropping the suit and coming back to him. He had his lawyers send her a copy, and when she read it, against the advice of her own counsel, she was moved. She dropped the suit and went back.

Her real name was Laura. In his stories, other than Maureen, it was Linda, Carol, Beth, Deirdre, and Sweetie Pie. In one story she went nameless, and in the novel her name was Emma Fairchild. But whatever the name it was always, unmistakably, her. She was the star of just about everything he wrote, and when she wasn't the star she made a cameo appearance; he gave her tiny walk-on parts, as though he were one of those nepotistic movie directors, the kind who employs his mistress and members of his family in every film he makes. But he wasn't a director; he was only a writer. Still, you knew who "the golden-haired girl" was when the narrator spotted her, even briefly, in the supermarket, or when, out of the corner of his eye, he spied a girl "with hair the color of sunshine."

For a period of time—almost overnight—he became famous, but then just as quickly drifted off into a puzzling obscurity.

His mother often wondered why he never wrote about her, and one day came out and asked him. He told her he was sorry, and promptly wrote a story with his mother in it, although everybody could tell it wasn't his mother at all, but Laura dressed up to look like his mother. It was the best he could do.

As for the woman, Laura, she loved him, she just thought he wrote too much. So he wrote about that. In this story he changed things around so that he was a salesman who was passionately devoted to his craft, but everything else was just about true to the facts, and it won a prize.

Then one day she got sick, and stayed that way for a long time. It was hard, but he wrote about it indirectly: Laura was absent from his stories now, but all his other characters became ill with something. They coughed a lot and took long naps. As she got sicker and sicker, so did everybody else in his other world, until finally nobody in any of his stories ever got out of bed. They were a bedridden lot, and his stories were very dull.

Finally, of course, she died.

After the funeral, he sat down at his desk, picked up a pencil, and wrote, *And then one day she died.*

He looked at what he had written, and he didn't like it. At all.

She died one day, he wrote.

But he didn't like that either.

So he erased it all and, in a flurry of inspiration, wrote, *She got real sick, but all of a sudden started feeling better.*

That was pretty good.

He had never seen her look so radiant.

Oh, yes!

And he lived, and she lived, and everybody lived happily ever after.

But that was a story.

The end.

WELCOME TO MONROE

On the morning of the seventh day, you knew they'd never find you. Not with dogs or with flashlights or with helicopters or handouts or all the men and women from town walking in lines through the woods so they wouldn't miss a thing. They would never find you because you couldn't be found. You were far away by then, somewhere near Monroe, Alabama. You knew that because that was the last sign you saw before he turned off that long stretch of main road. *Welcome to Monroe.* And the woods so deep and dark there, big enough to swallow the world. What a time for something like this to happen, days before Christmas, so close to Christmas that many of your presents were already wrapped and waiting beneath the tree. But this Christmas would be different from all the Christmases before it for your mother and your father and your brother and everyone who knew them, knew you. At school the teachers would take your friends aside and ask them questions, and then, when they began to cry, would let them talk to a man who knew what to say. The shadow of your absence would darken their world as your own world was darkened. But even so, you knew there would be other Christmases, and one day a long time away from this one all that had been fine and wonderful would be fine and wonderful again. Just not now and for some time to come.

Abernathy, your dog, had come the closest to finding you, and he was not even supposed to be looking. An old black-and-brown mutt who had wandered into your back-yard three years ago, you pleaded with you parents to let you keep him, and they had agreed, if you promised to take care of him. And you did, in your bedroom. The dog ate there and slept there beside you. Abernathy (named after your favorite uncle) was your dog, completely. He followed you to school and waited there and walked back with you. He had been there when you got in the man's car and watched as you drove away with him. He would not leave the corner where this happened, and when he was taken back home would return to that spot, day after day. He was still there, waiting, you were sure. The idea of it made you smile.

You could see things, even now, pictures of what was happening in your absence. It was amazing. You could see your house and your mother and father inside it and your brother in his room just lying on his bed looking at the ceil-ing and the pretty Christmas tree lights all dark and noth-ing now. But it wasn't clear really whether you were actually seeing it or were making up the pictures in your mind (or whatever your mind was now) from the crystal-clear mem-ories you had of everybody and your life with them. You knew them so well, better than you had ever imagined. Your mother spent most of the day frozen, barely breathing. She looked like one of those wax figures in a museum. She only got up to cook dinner for her husband and son; somehow the fact that she was taking care of them made her at least partly alive, although she herself didn't eat. *Eat something*, your father said. *Just a bite*. But no. Your dad left the house before sunrise every morning to look for you, wearing his tan windbreaker and the Crimson Tide baseball cap. He didn't go to work or even think about going to work. Your brother tried not to change at all, going out with his friends, playing basketball, talking to girls. But there was a hollowness beneath his eyes, and everyone treated him kindly, worried that any minute he might just break apart.

They would never find you. You knew what was happening to you, but they didn't, and this—the not-knowing—is what would haunt them. You knew that stories need an ending and that when they didn't have one people were unhappy. People like to read mysteries—you liked to read them—but they didn't like to have them in their lives, and that's what you were, would always be: a mystery. *The Mysterious Disappearance of Alyson McCrae*. Even a long time from now the mystery of your disappearance would occur to people you didn't even know, and they would wonder about it, and shake their heads. Without an ending there was always the possibility that what everyone thought happened hadn't, that you were somewhere in the world growing up, becoming a woman, living a life. As impossible as that was, there was always that possibility. That was your last and only wish: that they knew.

Never talk to strangers. That was the rule, and outside of the house it may have been the only rule, besides looking both ways before crossing the street, and you did both of them, without fail. But he wasn't a stranger. There were no strangers in your town; you knew almost everybody, more or less. You knew him less, but you knew him and he knew you, enough to call you by your full name: *Alyson Philadelphia McCrae.* Not everybody knew about the Philadelphia part. It was embarrassing, a ridiculous name you never understood. Your mom told you once it was where you were born, but you were born in Alabama, so that didn't make sense. *"Began* to be born, I said," she said. And then she smiled at you and rubbed your head. It was a pretty bad name though, and you never told anybody ("The *P* stands *for please mind your own business,"* you had been known to say), and so he must have heard it from your mom or dad. It was like saying a magic word—*abracadabra*—hearing him know this, assuming he knew your parents a lot better than he actually did. Though you pretended to be curious for a minute or two after, you never thought there could be anything wrong with getting in his car.

"Everybody's okay," he said. "But your mom and dad had to run down to Dothan all of a sudden."

"Grandma?" you said.

He nodded. "She's been better," he said. "All signs point to a swift recovery, however. They just needed to get down there and make sure the doctors don't bury her by accident."

"She's a wildcat," you said. "She'd scrape her way out, they did that."

"You'd better believe it," he said. "Car's right here. Hop on in."

"What about Abernathy?"

The man froze up and you couldn't figure out why. Now you know, of course. He thought there was somebody else there, somebody he didn't know about. "Who's Abernathy?" he asked.

"My dog," you said.

"Oh. Abernathy. I can't have a dog in the car," he said. "I'm allergic. Can Abernathy make his way back home on his own?"

"He's the smartest dog in Alabama," you said. And you held his small pointy head in your hands and kissed him right between the eyes. "You go on home now, Abernathy," you said. "Let's see who gets there first."

But Abernathy wouldn't move. He watched you get into the car and drive away, and when you turned around to look he was still there watching, getting smaller and smaller as you got farther and farther away.

How could no one have seen this? And not for you, because if they had it would have been way too late for you, but for your parents, for your brother, so they could have a place to set down their grief. In a town so small you knew everybody and everybody knew you. Maybe when everybody knows you they stop seeing you. Maybe you become invisible.

"This ain't the way home," you said. Now that you were in the car he figured he didn't have to pretend to be someone he wasn't, doing something he wasn't. He didn't have to pretend to be driving you home now.

"Maybe I know something you don't," he said.

"Like what?"

"Like maybe it's a shortcut."

"A longcut more like," you said. "You about can't get there from here."

"You sure have a mouth on you, Alyson Philadelphia McCrae," he said.

"Well, this ain't the way," you said.

"I think you'll see," he said, smiling over at you and driving, tapping the steering wheel with his index finger with a steady beat, as though he heard a song only he could hear.

You would see but by then it was way too late.

You kept trying to remember if you'd ever met him before as he drove out of town, past every farm you'd ever seen and then past those you hadn't. Maybe at a party your parents gave one time. That was it. "Alyson McCrae," he said. "It's a pleasure to meet you." You remembered now because he was an odd one. He was very skinny. He had a long face and right on top of it a forehead as big as Canada. His hair was thin too. You figure he had about eighteen hairs, all slicked back like they were worth the trouble. He had a small metal American flag pinned to the lapel of his jacket, which was brown. You thought you'd never seen him before but he knew your middle name so you figured there was something, some relationship, a bond between this man and your family, otherwise there is no way in the world you would have gotten into his car. No way in the world. But there was nothing you could do now.

"I don't know you," you said.

He was quiet now, driving, still drumming his finger against the steering.

"I want you to take me home," you said.

But it was as if you weren't even there.

On the morning of the seventh day you knew they'd never find you. But the truth is you really didn't know what day it was: it might have been the seven hundredth day, or the seven thousandth. Maybe everybody was dead, everybody you knew and everybody who knew you. Everybody was dead, and everybody died the same way, with the mystery inside of them, the mystery of what happened to Alyson Philadelphia McCrae.

Why? How long had you spent wondering why? What did you do that was so bad? How had you lived in the world that you would deserve to die like this? You reviewed every moment you could remember—and there were a lot of moments, twelve years of them—and you came up with nothing.

There was no reason. Things happened. Bad things, good things. Like Abernathy just wandering into the yard one day and becoming your warm and steady pal. And Janice, Maria, and Kristy, your three really good friends you'd never even met before this year. And the mother you had, and the father, and the brother—people who never let a whole day go by without letting you know in some way how much they loved you. What had you done to deserve all this sweetness?

Nothing. Things like this just happened. Nearly Christmas now, it seemed, and then that car, that man, that day. There was no real difference between the whys of the love and hate. Except the love was better.

THE MEN IN THE WOODS

The men who lived in the woods behind my house had been getting out of hand for some time. They were all in their mid-fifties, golfers formerly, and meat eaters—jolly men in general—but since their wives had sent them away to live in the woods they had become grumpy and discontent. At night they would bellow and howl. They wanted their televisions and ice makers and chairs beside the vents. They lived like animals in badly made straw huts and ate anything that wandered too close to their turf. We knew what was happening to our dogs and cats, but there was nothing we could do. Some of these men were very powerful; all of them belonged to the country club.

One night from a window I saw them leaving the woods and marching, single file, toward my home. They knocked at the door.

"What is it?" I said, staring at their wretchedness through the peephole. "What do you want?"

"Your telephone," they said. "We'd like to use your telephone."

"That's out of the question," I said. "You can't come in. My wife—"

"Your wife?" one of them said.

"She won't allow it."

"His wife won't allow it!" said another.

"His wife says no," said another.

"She must be wonderful," the first one said. "Really, I bet she is."

"She is," I said. "My wife is wonderful."

"We knew your father," one of the men said. "You're not your father."

Then they went away, grumbling, back into the woods.

Later, in bed, I told my wife what had happened.

"They came *here*?" she said. I nodded. She was appalled. "I want you to go down there and tell them not to do that. Tell them never to come here again."

"Now?" I said. "It's like, midnight."

"Now," she said. "For me."

She kissed me on the cheek.

I dressed and walked down the little trail that led to the woods behind our house. I saw a light and followed it. My heart was thumping against my ribcage and I almost turned back. But I reminded myself that I was doing this for my wife: acts of service were her love language. I saw them just up ahead. They were cooking squirrel around a fire and drinking coffee from old tin cups. They bellowed and wailed, but they seemed to be having a pretty good time.

"Hey fellas," I said, and all the bellowing stopped, and they looked up at me and smiled. "Please don't come around our house anymore. Okay?"

They looked at each other, then into the fire.

"Okay," they said, shrugging their shoulders. "Fine."

It didn't seem to mean that much to them. All they had wanted was the phone.

When I turned to go, I could see my house on the hill above me and watched as one light after another was killed, and it was all darkness. It seemed I could even hear the doors shut and lock as my wife prepared for sleep. My house seemed to disappear into the black sky. I paused.

"Going so soon?" one of the men said. The fire was bright, warm.

"Yeah," said another. "And just when we were getting to know you."

A WALK ON THE BEACH

We went out in the morning for one last walk together on the beach. I took his hand to steady him, to steady both of us, really. Knees are the first to go, they say, but the rest was not far behind. It was early, almost no one was there, and if you turned away from the rickety beach houses and sad hotels you could pretend you were on a deserted island.

"Isaac," I said, jostling his hand to get his attention. "Do you remember you told me once that when you were a kid you always wanted to live on a deserted island because you thought that meant it was just chock full of desserts?"

The sun was rising behind a sheet of thin clouds, but a ray slipped through and made our morning shadows. Even his face—the dried, crevassed creases like a rain-starved plain—brightened into a darkness.

"Remember, honey?"

He was looking down at his bare feet for some reason, but I knew he had heard me and was thinking about it, trying so hard. There was always a lag now between a question and an answer, like the delay on a long-distance call. For fifty years he was the sharpest tack I ever knew. Now he needed me just to find his shoes in the morning, to explain to him the subtle differences between a fork and a spoon, to double-lock the doors at bedtime so he couldn't escape into the night. It had become too much for me. Rather, *he* had become too much for me.

"I don't remember that," he said.

"It was nothing," I said, giving his hand a little squeeze. "Just funny is all."

"It does sound like something a kid would say, though." He looked at me and smiled, friendly but guarded, as if we'd been talking just for the last few minutes instead of the last fifty years. "And I was never a good speller. I let other people do the spelling for me."

"You hired the best spellers in the business."

"That's right."

Now a laugh from him, and a laugh from me. I wanted to tell him how happy it made me that he'd kept his sense of humor, but then he would ask what I meant. *Tell me about the things I've lost.* So I didn't say anything and just listened to our laughter carried away by the wind.

The water lapped at our ankles and so I led us a little ways away from the surf for more solid ground. Everything in the world conspired to knock you over.

He kept staring at his feet. They looked like blue-veined sea creatures, the kind that lived miles beneath the water, the kind that sometimes washed ashore and made you wonder how such a thing could ever even be in the world. And why.

"I could live in this town," he said, "if it weren't for the earthquakes and fires and floods, and pestilences."

"You do live here, silly."

"Well then wish me luck!"

"Oh, you've always been lucky."

He snuck a shy glance at me. Tentative, searching.

"And you. You live here too?"

"I do," I said.

"But we don't live together."

"No. Not anymore. Not like we used to. But I'll be there so often you'll think we did. At your new place."

He nodded, as if this were an acceptable answer.

We kept walking and he looked down again and for some reason it irritated me.

"Why in the world do you keep looking at your feet?"

"My feet?" No pause this time. His fog was lifting. "Ha! I'm not looking at my feet. I'm looking for a shark's tooth. I've been hoping to find a shark's tooth every time I come to the beach for, I don't know, sixty-five years? But I never have."

"Oh." I didn't know that for some reason. "Another regret?"

"No, no," he said. "No. I'm glad I've never found one. Hoping is better. You know, because when you do find it— presto-change-o!—you're hopeless."

"Then you just have to hope for other things."

"Like what?"

He was right. The list of things to hope for was getting shorter, almost every day.

A woman in an unfortunate bathing suit, a sunburned man with a beach chair on his back, two boys running into the surf screaming like Maori warriors attacking the whole ocean, a jogger and her snow-white poodle. We had not walked far but I didn't know how much farther we should. Going out was the easy part but then we'd have to go back and that was so much harder. My hip was throbbing already. I wished we had a limo following behind us at just a bit of a distance so that we could get into when we wanted to. With a limo driver named Norman. That was something to hope for, I suppose.

"I don't think there's a god," he said out of nowhere, "but if there were all I would want from him or her is just a little direction. Hints. Like, *Warm, warmer, warmer—you're burning up!* Or, say you're about to quit your job and he says, *Cold! Cold!* Just that, a couple of words. That would be nice, right?"

"That would be ideal," I said.

He stopped and turned to me and took both of my hands in his and if you were looking at us from a distance you'd swear this old man was about to propose.

"That place looks like an elementary school with a shitty cafeteria," he said.

"I tried to get you a room in the Taj Mahal, but they were full up."

"Don't be a bitch," he said. "Don't be a real bitch."

He loved that word now. I don't know why. I had to just let it go.

"Do you have a cigarette?"

"Cold," I said, shaking my head. "Really cold. You quit in 1995."

"I never quit, I just stopped. I have pursued secondhand smoke for years."

He winked at me. This man. We kept walking. I untwined my fingers from his to brush the hair from my face and it freaked him out, and he pulled my arm down until he found my hand again and held it like a vise.

"Marriage vows should be different than they are, I was thinking," he said. His voice rose a bit and shook. "Not until *death* do us part. Just until the other loses his mind. Only *then* may you leave."

These moments of perfect clarity, of understanding, they astonished me and made me sadder than almost anything else.

"I am not leaving you."

"One of us is leaving the other. And it's not me."

No, I thought, a thought that was truer than I wanted it to be: it's you, it's definitely you. I didn't say it. But there were so many things I couldn't say anymore. I listened to the static of the frosted, frothy waves instead. He stopped and turned to the horizon, where there was nothing to see except the place where everything disappeared.

"I want a Viking funeral. Set me on a wooden raft, float me out to sea."

"But you're not dying, Richard. Not. Dying." Sometimes he drove me insane. "You were a kind of Viking though. Brave, strong, a good breadwinner, but also plundering and burning stuff down."

"Plundering," he said, and shook his head, as if it were a riddle he couldn't figure out. "Are you sure? I don't remember any plundering, Sara. Not a bit of it. I'm sorry."

And then just like that we found ourselves stuck calf-deep in the stealthy rising tide. We couldn't move for a second. He gripped my hand and he looked at me with such helplessness, his eyes as scared and wild as a child's. Then the ocean disappeared, and we were free.

I felt the sun starting to burn. It was time. I led him back to the dunes where we'd left his shoes, but they weren't there. I scanned the beach. All the dunes looked the same now, graves for ancient mariners with the sea oats waving in the wind.

"I can't find your shoes," I said.

"*You* can't find my shoes? That's new."

"It's just, I thought they were right here. But maybe they're up the beach a little."

"Maybe," he said. "Maybe not."

His eyes were swimming, all the maybes and may-be-nots bouncing around in his brain.

"I guess this means we can't go now," he said, grinning at me like a little boy, my lifelong conspirator, my partner in crime.

But that's not what it meant. I saw them down the way.

CHAMPIONS OF LITERATURE

You remember how Josephine prayed. She was always praying. I don't know why she prayed at a writers conference, but I got the feeling she prayed before doing anything. I closed my eyes and pretended I was too. Who would know different but God, who didn't have a dog in the hunt anyway? I heard an old Hall and Oates song in my head instead, the bouncy one that makes everybody dance. Long before Josephine said *Amen*, I opened my eyes and saw yours were open too. This is how we met: while everyone else was praying. Josephine asked each of us to say a few words about writing and how others might learn to write and what it meant to be a writer and if we wrote in the morning or late at night. You, (the poet), went first, I (the story writer) went second, and the man who wrote books about unsolved murders (true crime) went third. Questions?

At lunch Josephine told us stories about her summers on the Gulf, the jellyfish, the first paved roads, the church her great-grandfather built with three free Black men a hundred years ago—swallowed by a sinkhole just last year. No one was hurt. You didn't laugh, because a church built by three free Black men swallowed by a sinkhole isn't funny. "Oh, Josephine," you said, and held her hand, which happened to be resting beside the sweaty water glass on your side of the table. "That is almost unbelievably terrible," I said. The true crime writer took a note. It was only later, after Josephine dropped us off at the writers' hotel and the true crime writer left us, that you fell against the stucco walls on the open walkway leading to your room and laughed so hard you started shivering. You ended up sitting down, back against wall, trying to recover. I picked you up. I had known you for three hours, but I picked you up, hands beneath your arms. "They say sinkholes are the quicksand of our time," you said.

We were on a panel in a half-empty classroom where we gave our "talk" to the old, the retired, the eager, and, I'm pretty sure, the unhoused people who come to these things. Josephine moderated. You talked about Black women poets, and I talked about family, because apparently that's all I write about. The true crime writer talked about how truly depraved people could be. There were nine people there. No one asked questions, they just said what they thought and wanted to hear what we thought about what they thought. *All of your characters are so full of longing*, one woman said. We waited for the rest but all she said was, *I'd like to hear what all of you have to say about that.* The true crime writer said, *Longing for longer lives, you bet.* You said, *I think all peo-*

ple, and maybe especially Black people, live in a state of constant longing. Then it was my turn. *I don't know what you mean by longing*, I said. It came out sounding smart-alecky and writer-like, though I hadn't meant it to. A little jarring. *Oh, you know what she means*, you said. I turned to you, far away at the other end of the fold-out table. You looked at me like we had talked about this a million times.

✳ ✳ ✳ ✳

We had a drink together at the hotel bar before going to the writers' party. You said, *My husband watches me disappear into the basement and every couple of years come up with a bunch of poems. He's not sure what happens or how it happens or whether it's a good thing, but he reads them and says he loves them, all of them, each and every one.* I said, *I don't have to disappear, but it takes me longer.* You smiled. *Longer*, you said. *Long, longer, longing. See what I did there?* And I would have said something, I had a riposte in my pocket, but the true crime guy was there and it was time to get into someone's big old car and drive to the house of the woman who was throwing the party for the writers. We all got to go together, walked outside into the Florida night, surprisingly chilly. *It's so cold*, you said, *and me without a coat.* I sat in the backseat and stared at the back of your head. You never turned around to look at me but occasionally you'd look at the true crime guy and I could catch your profile edged against the lights of oncoming cars. Your face looked like the coast of a country with a long, dark history. I wrote this in my mind and thought, *I should put that in a story*, but then I decided not to because it sounded like something I would put in a story. It took fifteen minutes to get out to this lady's house and after a while you turned around to me and said, *We can hear you thinking.* Then the true crime guy said, *I was wondering what that sound was.* Everyone laughed.

It had been a cabin once, this place, and over the years turned into a model home. The walls in the living room were of dark, varnished pine, and the heads of animals kept watch above us, nobly dead. Wine in plastic cups, cheese, crackers, grapes. It was hard to hear anything in the tipsy hubbub. I followed you around like a dog. I didn't know where the true crime guy had gone. A couple of times you caught my eye and said something with them, cracking a smile, that thing people who knew each other do, but I'd only known you six or seven hours at this point and played it safe, and offered a noncommittal nod. Josephine waved at us, but she was too far, cornered in a crowd, and couldn't get over. You winked at her.

We'd been asked to introduce ourselves to the hostess, Mrs. Murphy, a champion of literature. A widow, snow-white hair, big pearls, warm, gray eyes. She was so nice and treated us as if we had a pedigree. She took our hands in her own—one each, as though she were leading horses into a stall, took us to her bedroom and closed the door and the din behind it died. *This is where I live, for the most part*, she said. She had a big fat bed with wooden bedposts and doilies on her bedside table. On the other side a stack of books high as a third grader. I saw my book and I saw yours. None by the true crime guy. The room was full of fresh flowers and on top of her dresser a herd of ceramic animals, elephants and zebras, but others more exotic, like a mandrill. You could see the outline of her body on the bed, where she spent her life reading. And the window looking out into a garden. There was something perfect about this room. *Can we live with you?* you said, laughing, and I laughed, but Mrs. Murphy did not. She was old and sweet and a little crazy. *Of course you can, dear*, she said, and I really think she meant it. *That would be lovely.* And she looked from me to you. *But don't you have a home of your own, a family?* We did, of course. Just not the same ones.

* * * *

We went back to the hotel together, hitching a ride with a reader. You invited me to your room for a drink and I said maybe I'll just go to bed, and you said okay. I gave you my book and you used it as a doorstop. *In case you change your mind*, you said, *I have half a bottle of cheap white wine in the fridge.*

I changed my mind. A few minutes later I walked into your room. I didn't see you. I said your name, but you didn't answer. There was your open suitcase, socks spilling over the top, caught in mid-escape. A laptop with a dark screen. A candy bar. You were out on the balcony, smoking a cigarette, the sliding glass door open a crack. The moon lit up the world, and though there was a beach and an ocean out there all I could see was you, and I wanted you to turn around and see me too. But you didn't. You smoked your cigarette, and the smoke was rushed away by the wind, and you stood on your tiptoes looking out at something remarkable, your hair flying like a flag of your own little country. Then I heard you laugh, and the wind took that away too.

RUNNING

The next morning he went for a run. He'd never spent the night with her before and wasn't familiar with the neighborhood, and running was the way he learned about a place. The man had done this on business trips in Iowa City, Boise, Des Moines, working for a small company selling genetically modified corn seed. He'd done it after being with other women too—not all that often, but often enough. He was thirty-four years old and strong with a great mane of black hair and thought he might be the freest person who had ever lived.

He stretched and worked up a little sweat by sort of hopping, sort of dancing on the street corner. He glanced over his shoulder and wondered if he could see the window of her apartment, if maybe she was watching him now. He couldn't see her. Then he took off. The first two blocks were all retail: jewelers and Chinese wholesale and flower shops and tobacconists. But after taking a right, three blocks straight on, the crumbling city seemed to disappear behind him. Around him now were weed-choked lots, an abandoned home, cement blocks, and old car tires stacked in unsteady towers. Then he took a left down what appeared to be an alley. There was a dog there, a perfect, terrible monster of a dog, black and thick shouldered. It seemed to be grinning, grinning with its sharp teeth bared as it approached, tentatively at first, but then leaping, just missing the man's left arm.

The monster growled in a low rumble. It lunged at him again, and then again. It came so close the man could see its teeth, its dark pink gums, and he drew back a step, and another. Then he remembered that an animal would see this as a sign of weakness, so when the dog came at him again the man stood his ground and growled himself. Still the dog charged at him so he kicked it, hard, just below its right eye, and the dog retreated, but not so far that the man could get past it. The man turned and went back the way he came. He could feel his heart beating in his ears. He ran back to the city. He passed the woman's apartment building. But something made him stop and look. This time he saw her clear as day at the high window, smiling at him broadly. It must have been the light. He could see her hair, her eyes, the curve of her cheek. He could even see her teeth. Had she been there all this time, waiting for him? She waved, and he lifted his hand. He saw he'd been cut—bitten. The blood ran across his palm in a shallow stream and left a rusty trail. The sight of blood made him lightheaded. Still, he took the stairs to her apartment two at a time and ran through the open door and surprised himself by almost falling into her arms. He showed her his hand.

"Oh, baby," she said. "Let me fix it."

He hadn't known he needed fixing, until then.

THE LADDER

She kept the ladder hidden against the far side of the house, on its side, behind an array of shrubbery and a small pyramid of partially charred firewood. It was a metal ladder, and heavy, yellow and blue, and picking it up involved several challenging moves—lifting, leaning, pushing, and prying it into its sturdy inverted *V*. Harder now than ever but still doable. The hinges adjoining the two sides of the ladder sometimes stuck, and with her bare hands she had to *thwonk* them until they were perfectly straight. The meaty part of her palm had been pinched more than once during the course of this procedure; her Saran Wrap–thin skin roughly torn like a child's scraped knee. All of this happened at night, in almost complete darkness, the only light from the dim bulb in the laundry room, casting a soft, milky glow through the dusty windows onto the thorny leaves of a winterberry. Once the ladder was open she shook it, made sure the ground was level. Usually she'd have to adjust it, moving the legs this way and that a few times before it felt secure. Then she climbed, step by step, testing her balance on each flat rung, falling into a worry that made her take special care not to slip or get her slacks caught on anything. It was especially dangerous when she got to the very top, where it was written in serious, Ten Commandant letters: THIS IS NOT A STEP. Here there was a sharp metal protrusion, the final test that she had, so far, nimbly passed. She got on her knees on the step that wasn't, and with her forearms on the shingles drug herself onto the sloping edge of the roof, turned herself around, and sat, breathing. She brushed the dirt off her forearms. Another breath and she was fully there.

This is what she did for her cigarette, the only one she allowed herself, once a night every night, for almost all her adult life. She didn't even have to hide it anymore, because there was no one here to secret it from. But it had become a part of who she was, a tradition she could not and would not and did not want to end until she couldn't make the climb. It was necessary. It was her spot, her perch. There was no great view to be had, really, just the cross-the-street neighbors, a young couple in the modest, red-brick split-level, their lives ahead of them, as they say, as if all our lives weren't ahead of us, some just farther along than others. Sometimes she could see them—the Shambergers?—as they moved from room to room, miniature people, busy as little ants. It was like watching a movie from a thousand feet away.

She smoked, and the smoke rose and quivered from the red and orange coal into a dreamy cloud, then off into a dreamy nothing. But most of the smoke was inside her, in her lungs and her blood. It made its way to her brain and she felt lighter, lighter. She felt like she could follow the smoke if she wanted. The cigarette didn't last very long, never as long as she wanted it to, but always time enough to review the plot points of her life, the highlights, good and bad, the husband and the children and now the grands, the cars, the planes, the ships, the glam, and the struggle, the love, the sex, so much of it really it didn't seem fair that one woman should have it all. So much. But every night she climbed the ladder's rungs and sat here, here on top of the world, smoking, she wondered what it meant that out of all of it, out of every single second she remembered, this was the best, the very best, the moment she lived for, surrounded by the invisible world beneath the moon and long dead stars, sharing her own light with the dark.

FIRST IN, LAST OUT

On our last day at the beach the sun came out, and the fog, which for that whole week had draped the shore in a veil of cotton, burned away, and we discovered there was an ocean here after all. It wasn't blue, really, closer to black, but when the waves flattened out across the beach the water was perfectly clear, and full of minnows and tiny crabs. The shells were just so-so, mostly shards of something that used to be beautiful, like ancient pottery washed up from the ocean floor, there to remind you the world was old. It just felt good to have the sun on our shoulders as my wife and I—so young, newlyweds, in point of fact—walked across the warming sand, hand in hand. She was wearing a black two-piece, simple and very small. Her hair (thick, dark chocolate brown) was in pigtails, and somehow this girlish maneuver heightened her brazen but effortless display of pure, glorious womanhood. I was invisible and in the best possible way.

"I'm glad our honeymoon wasn't ruined," she said.

I stopped walking and looked at her. "I didn't know it was even close to being ruined," I said. "We've made love like a hundred times, read three novels, and binged an entire season of *The Walking Dead*. And the plague is over. That's almost perfect."

"Yeah," she said. "I didn't mean *ruined*. But you can't go back and tell people that it was foggy and it rained the whole time and you read and watched TV. It sounds gloomy."

"You skipped the part about making love."

"Because you can't tell people that."

"No," I said. "Let's tell them it was sunny every day and we swam with the dolphins."

"But that's a lie and that—that would be wrong," she said, and we laughed. Somehow this had become a joke: saying *but that would be wrong* after every wrong thing we talked about doing. I have no idea why or how but it was hilarious to us, *just to us*, the way that something that clearly isn't funny becomes funny for reasons impossible to explain. "That being said, I'll totally never forget that ride we took on the humpbacked whale."

How long had we been walking? I had no idea. I stopped and looked behind us: I couldn't see our hotel or any landmark at all. Civilization had disappeared behind the curve of the shore. I could imagine that we were on a deserted island, looking toward the horizon for a rescue we knew would never come. I don't know what she was thinking, but she had that faraway look in her eyes as well, and as I looked into them (her eyes were the color of ivy) the tail end of a wave chilled my toes. I almost gasped it was so cold.

She turned to me.

"I'm going in," she said.

"No way."

"I could never live with myself if I went to the beach and didn't get in. I would be ashamed for the rest of my life. You're coming in too."

"I don't think so."

"You're my husband now," she said. "You have to. It was in our vows."

"Those vows were ambiguous."

"On purpose, for occasions like this."

She let go of my hand and took a deep breath, girding herself. I took a step toward the water myself but with her hand on my stomach she held me back.

"I'm first in," she said. "I'm always first in. Ever since I was little. That's what I want on my tombstone: *First In, Last Out*. Remember that."

"I will."

"I'm serious," she said, and she studied my face. "You'll remember?"

"I'll remember. But I didn't know that about you."

"Well," she said. "I guess there's a lot you don't know about me."

"Oh? Like what?"

But she was already gone. She ran into the water as fast as she could, whooping, slowing as the water got deeper. She pushed into it with her legs until she couldn't walk at all and then dove under, disappearing for what seemed like a long time. She resurfaced about five yards out, the bigger waves rolling against her back, lifting and releasing her, up and down, up and down. I think she was smiling.

We'd planned a big wedding, with friends and family coming in from all over. There was going to be a band and your choice of chicken or fish or veg, and a first dance and a sound system that could turn even my mousey, eighty-year-old Aunt Muriel's voice into that of a roaring lion. But all that was postponed, of course. We'd talked about waiting, to do what we'd hoped to do but just a little bit later. *When things got back to normal.* But we couldn't wait. We were married at the courthouse, with our two best friends, witnesses to our contract, safe behind a plexiglass wall. Now here we were at the beach, in the days just before summer, the rest of our lives ahead of us. Six days of fog and rain, one day of sun, and then the rest of our lives.

She waved, I waved.

"Come and get me if you dare!" she yelled into the wind, my freckled goddess in the wine-dark sea, the woman who had already told me the words she wanted on her tombstone when death does us part. I wanted to tell her what I wanted on mine too, but the water was cold, and she was already so far away.

[DUST JACKET COPY, UNREVISED]

Makayla Katz is the author of three novels. Essays and opinion pieces by Katz have appeared in *The Guardian*, *Salon*, *Elle*, *Sassy Pants*, and elsewhere, and her extemporaneous pastoral poems have been shared widely on the Internet. Her novels have been nominated for many awards, including but not limited to some of the bigger ones every writer wants to be nominated for. Last year she received the Silver Cord, a prize given to writers who, after a certain point, are still alive. Katz now resides in a small enclave near a medium-sized metropolitan area, alone.

Katz was born in 1961 in New York City. She remembers little from her Big City days—mostly smells. Sulfur? Exhaust? A long-neglected dumpster in the alley behind the old homeplace? Some sounds too: was it laughter? Or a sort of high-pitched and breathless moan—a wailing? Unclear. The game-changing moment for Katz happened when she was three months old: an icicle fell from a skyscraper's window ledge, into her stroller, piercing the secondhand baby carriage like an assassin's dagger. Closer to her rubbery body by half an inch, they say, and it would have plunged through

her ribcage and into her little baby heart with ease. She remembers the moment vividly. But does she, really? Is it instead a memory she's created, having been told this story
over a hundred times, and told it herself a hundred more?
Will she ever know?

She doesn't think she will.

Post-icicle, family lore was born: she survived for a reason. Great things to come for the little one, they said. Not
great fame or fortune or luck in love (yet). But something.
Waiting for the jury to come back with the verdict on this
one. One thing is true: as soon as she could hold a mark-mak-
ing instrument she wrote down sounds and words and drew
pictures, for which she received quiet encouragement from
her parents—something between a pat on the head and a
grudging half-hug. There was some indefinable something
in her work. Everybody saw it. She was writing poetry before
she knew what poetry even was. Katz would never say this of
herself, though she totally believed it: she was a born writer.

The Katz family—Mother, Father, scribbling little
Makayla—moved from the big city to smaller ones in Florida, Alabama, Maine, Tennessee, California, and Oregon, all
before she was ten years old. Not that Katz noticed: her face
was in one book after another. She could have been on Mars,
for all she cared. Financial opportunities were everywhere
but seemed to vanish just as the Katz family approached.
When she was eleven, they moved to Riverside, Indiana, to
live with and care for an ailing relative. It was a boxy house

on a sylvan street. The relative kept to her room, making only occasional noises. Katz's mother and father seemed to care for her as best they could, bringing her food and water, pretzels, cookies, et cetera; she had, they said, "a condition." Katz saw her only once. It was in the middle of the night. Katz had awoken from a dream, her mouth dry and sticky. She needed a glass of water. The house was so quiet and dark. As she stepped into the hallway she saw the ailing relative, sublimely ancient and gray, miniature, no bigger than Makayla was herself. The ailing relative seemed just as surprised as she to see another human in the hallway. Slowly the old woman raised an arm, her clawed, gaunt fingers appearing to cling to the air itself. She was wearing a nightgown covered in rose petals, and in interviews decades later Katz would often insist that she could see right through her—though, again, that seems implausible.

Her father, Eckhart Katz, was an inventor who dabbled in concrete. He created a revolutionary solution so durable it could hold bridges together with a filament as thin as a spider's web. Changed the landscape of bridge building forever but then partnered with a shyster who stole his patent and left the family with nothing. Eckhart Katz went on to invent a brand-new kind of lickable glue used on the backs of postage stamps, universally adopted, but partnered with another shyster who left the family with even less.

Her mother, Anna, had dreams of becoming an artist but had given it all up to be an inventor's wife. On fire with ideas her husband was, on *fire* with new ways to make life on Earth better for everybody—everybody, that is, other than his wife and daughter. They had it hard. Most of his eureka moments seemed to come late at night. He hardly ever slept. Katz remembers his hulking, unshaven presence, wide-shouldered in an undershirt, a sweet and gentle giant of a man, kind of crazy, experimenting with this and that at the breakfast table, building models of his designs (the Self-Cleaning Birdhouse™ resists forgetting). It would not be surprising for young Makayla to find a wing nut in her Lucky Charms. He was either on the verge of something great or enduring a dramatic setback. Katz was fond of her father but his manic energy frightened her too and is probably the reason she is skittish around men to this very day. Much of her work interrogates love and fear and how inseparable the two emotions are, to her at least.

The ailing relative did not live long, and though nothing hinky appears to have occurred the Katz family did not advertise the death widely and stayed on in the now more expansive home for some of the best years of their lives.

In Riverside her father somehow became the superintendent of parks and recreation. He invented, among many other unique and stillborn creations, the first portable basketball court, and just before he died was drawing up plans for using an invisible mesh to capture falling leaves *before* they hit the ground. He would have died in his sleep had he ever been able to sleep; instead, he died with his eyes wide open in his bedroom after dinner. No one knew he was dead for some time. Turns out death looks a lot like someone having an idea.

Katz was fifteen at the time; her mother was thirty-four. Katz took it in stride, burying whatever grief she felt beneath a stratum of callused feelings or un-feelings, and moving on. But his death, like a broken spell, transformed her mother. After a few weeks of "mourning" (that is, cigarettes and bourbon) she became, for the first time in her life, happy. A happy woman. Such happiness. Life was a gift she had never opened. She wore loose-fitting blouses and painted fanciful murals of Italian country life across the walls of their possibly inherited home, on every wall in every room, until there was not a blank space to be found, just green, rolling, Umbrian hills and grape-stomping peasants and herds of wild deer and boars. While watching her mother change in this way, Katz may have surmised that it was in the absence of men women were truly content. That's where all the evidence pointed, anyway. Why do women work so hard to get a man, as it's clearly against their own interests? Somehow they can't help themselves and that's probably because: babies. Women wanted babies. At fifteen Katz herself vowed never to have a child and thus would cure herself of men. She would become a writer and be content from the get-go.

Fast-forward two years! Seventeen. Martin Hoffman arrived halfway through senior year. Rangy and unkempt as a scarecrow, shy as a puppy, he was delivered to Riverside to rattle her. Appeared one day in the office of the *Screaming Eagle* (high school newspaper) and inquired with the editor—Makayla Katz—if he could be of any service. He claimed not to be much of a writer, so she put him in charge of selling ads. Showed him the ropes. There were sparks—or, scratch that. More a glow than sparks. Steam heat. Awkward at first, finding their way into it all like two blind children lost in the woods. How to converse? What to do with your arms? This urge to bite him: what was that? Good thing, bad? She wanted to bite him for the longest time. Eventually, she did. There was so much life in her life now that she wanted to die. She couldn't take it. And then the charms he left for her in the crooked roots of a sweet gum tree. Letters of love. Then actual love. Young love. The best love and the very very worst. She made mixtape CDs of the soundtrack of her love for him and slipped them into his backpack when he wasn't looking. The musical message: you are my one and only forever and ever.

As insurance, she made copies. One or two may have found their way into other backpacks. She simply didn't know what it meant to be true and never really learned. She became a wanderer, a hobo of the heart, alighting anywhere she pleased, like a fly on a pizza. Martin responded in kind, making the rounds, becoming a minor sexual celebrity in his own right. Whatever. Higher education took them hundreds of miles away from Riverside, from each other. But that night before they packed their separate cars and drove away they met beneath that old sweet gum tree with a bottle of wine and a Dixie cup and it was like old times, and each swore eternal devotion to the other. Some days later she took it all back. That sweet gum tree, it made you say some things you maybe didn't mean.

Katz returned to Riverside with a degree in French and cursive writing, back with her mother in the home of her once-ailing relative. Martin visited now and again. He lived far away, in the city, doing quite well selling ads for a glossy magazine. *Ummmm thank you, Makayla?* Nope. Never heard an ounce of gratitude from Martin. For God's sakes. He was invited over to dinner at Christmastime because Anna Katz (always a fan of Martin) insisted, and as they spooned Tuscan white bean soup into their pie holes Katz tried to ignite a spark in her heart, in her loins, anywhere, but all she felt was a spinal quiver way past its use-by date, and a distant melody she had to bend her ear to hear. She hugged him when he left and it was like hugging the mailman. And that was the end of that.

This experience was the foundation for her first novel, *The Thankless Salesman.*

Time passed. Katz wrote, published a story or two in *Scrimshaw* and *The Combustible Umbrella.* She made a kind of living selling jewelry made of her inventor father's leftover parts. She wore long flowy dresses and fell in with a printmaker, more than slightly older than she was. Bald with a prehensile rat tail (like if you pulled it, it would ring a little bell), a tiny man with a long face. He was quick to smile, to laugh, and overly fond perhaps of uttering tea-bag-inspired truisms: *Life is a chance. Love is infinity. Grace is reality.* She had a harmless affection for the tiny printmaker, but it was a flimsy attachment that would not move mountains. They moved to a shed in the country. He had this thing he did too, or didn't do, what he called an *idiosyncrasy*: he slept with all his clothes on. Everything but his shoes. She asked him, *Trauma? Birthmark*, he said. He told her he had a big birthmark, undeniably grotesque, covering great swaths of his body. Had never shown his birthmark to anybody. Nobody? Nobody. Katz of course worked as hard as she could to get him to show it to her, harder maybe than she had ever worked for anything in her life. She wanted to be the one, the first, possibly the only ever. It wasn't about love, exactly, or trust; it was just enough of a goal to keep this tepid romance alive because starting over is *exhausting*. She showed him her collection of flaws: toes, slightly webbed; tiny bald spot above her left ear; "and face it," Katz said, "my incisors look like fangs, like I vant to suck your blood" (unavoidably harkening back to Martin and the biting, biting, biting: sigh).

It worked; he compromised. Night after pitch dark night he shed a single piece of clothing. After a week he was down to one sock and a night later was as God made him.

A week or two later he turned on the lights.

He showed her.

And he was right. The birthmark was truly grotesque.

It was less a birthmark, really, than it was a curse. Something he should have seen a doctor about a long time ago, before it took over his body like—like—well, it was not like anything. But okay. What was it like. It was like if someone had spilled a giant cup of strawberry milk on him and he was a paper towel, or the birthmark was an alien and he was its human host. Katz felt so superficial. She couldn't touch it. She couldn't touch him. Ever. Again.

He should never have shown her the birthmark. Katz told him that. "Your instincts were right," she said. "Never show this birthmark to anybody again. It's not . . . good."

He seemed bereft for a moment, almost wounded. Then he remembered a couple of teabags. *The gate to happiness is self-compassion*, he said. And: *Walk beautifully, talk beautifully, live beautifully.*

She wished it were as simple as that, and maybe it was.

He forgave her, but it didn't matter. She was not much longer for the shed.

Before the big reveal, though, before the end of it all, every morning she would sneak out while he was sleeping and walk to the nearby pond and sit beside its froggy water and watch the sun rise. And as it did, as its light gradually spread across the water and the land as jittery fluorescent lights illuminate the show floor of a department store moments before opening, Katz wrote and wrote. In one spiral-bound notebook after another. She felt it; something was happening on these pages, these horizontally blue-lined pages with the red vertical stripes, something suggesting order, something that both guided her elsewhere and hemmed her in. Which is exactly what she needed, really: ordering and hemming. They were the same type of spiral-bound notebooks she'd used in grade school, in high school, and in her first year of college. By the time she was a sophomore she purchased a computer, which was awesome, but her writing on it was soulless. It was an infinite pallet without guard rails or gravity. She wrote stories that bounced through time and space with recklessness, and nothing was alive, ever, not even a word, not even a comma. She wrote dead things; she was a creator of literary corpses. She concluded that it was probable that her passion was not commensurate with her talent, which just meant that as much as she wanted to she probably just couldn't do it.

Returning to the notebooks turned things around, though. Look at them all! So many notebooks! She thought she had something.

When the sun fully cleared the top of the pines she headed back to the shed and climbed in bed with the disastrously naked printmaker. But she couldn't sleep, and rose, packed her notebooks and left the shed and didn't look back except once when she heard a twig snap and thought maybe he was creeping up behind her, that he loved her too much to let her go, that she would be a captive in the shed until she died: *Love is an experience to infinity*, he would say, drinking a cup of tea, watching her breathe.

But it wasn't the printmaker; it was a doe, her big, black, wet eyes like ink puddles reflecting the last light of a crescent moon. Katz turned, walked faster into the gathering light of day.

She had, as noted, always been a little skittish around men. Because of her father, she always said, a man who left his nuts and bolts in her milk and Lucky Charms.

The truth? Her father was a convenient excuse for her inability to love anything at all, other than writing, other than reading, other than the imaginary worlds she could invent or escape into. Waxing on about her mornings by the pond writing in the fresh light of day with the song of the birds and the lament of the frogs as her soundtrack—as if nature itself were no more than her backup singer, the sun a spotlight for her performance. On her tombstone, if she ever dies, should be these words: *Though spared by the frozen dagger, her heart was cold.* Which sounds sad but, really, is okay with her.

So to say Katz left the printmaker because of his birthmark is, obviously, inaccurate.

(Though it was horrendous.)

She left because he had shown her all of him and there was nothing there left to see.

This experience provided the grist for her second novel, bravely entitled *The Printmaker's Birthmark*.

She wrote *Birthmark* between shifts giving change and selling miniature boxes of detergent to indigent college students at the Ram's Plaza Automat, where she lived in the storage room. Men and women came into her life and sooner than one thought possible they disappeared. One stayed on for a while, taking advantage of Katz's access to so much free detergent. In the end she made no lasting connections and very few fleeting ones. Writing, Katz feels, is the most human of all the arts: it's how we speak to each other, how we come to know each other. And yet, as she will be the first to tell you, she doesn't like humans very much at all. Which in and of itself is interesting to her and something she will no doubt write about one day, for those same humans to read.

One morning she awoke to discover that the automat had gone out of business, the heavy glass doors locked from the outside: the owners had never known she lived there. Exiting through an alley-facing window she landed in a trash can full of rancid meat, coffee grounds, and stale bread, which was comic, she thought, but only when it happens to other people.

Suddenly she was homeless, unhoused, free of a home, home-free. After hours "on the street" she moved back in with her old mother, who seemed genuinely happy her daughter had come home. They connected in ways they never had when Katz was growing up, more like sisters, now, who told each other everything. Two months later—two months later to the day—her mother died. *Unbelievable*. Died in her sleep. Cancer. Her mother had left her a letter on her bureau. Turns out she had known she was dying for a while but kept it to herself. Wanted the last times with the person she loved most to be normal, to be real. No tears, no pity, just the playing of cards and the taking of walks, remembering the past together—her brilliant, somewhat crazy husband, who was also Katz's brilliant, somewhat crazy father. This and that. A reviewing.

Conclusion: good outweighed the bad.

But it was bad for a bit when Katz's mother died. Katz felt something—grief? It may have been grief. A crack of the heart. She was an orphan now, after all. But it turned out to be more like a mosquito bite, a mosquito bite on her back between her shoulder blades, impossible to reach, impossible to scratch. Maddening. Intolerable from time to time, but eventually diminishing and finally going away forever.

Katz now lives in the boxy home on the sylvan street. It's a fine home, better than Katz feels she deserves. There is that room, though, the room where three people died: the ailing relative, her father, and her mother. Katz stays out of that room for quite a while, and only after a heaping amount of time has passed does she have the guts to enter. Musty, mothballed memories. In the closet are her father's threadbare suits, her mother's peasant skirts. And what's this? On the floor of the closet is a smallish wooden box, handmade, old as time. It's the kind the captain of a schooner might use to store precious items from the mainland, such as pictures of his wife and family, his father's pocket watch, the Bible. But this box is full of scraps of paper, a few words scrawled on each. *Everyone is gone*, one reads. And, *Where is my family?*

And, *Who are these people in my home?* Dozens and dozens of these little scraps of paper. Katz sifts through the dusty collection and eventually realizes they belonged to the ailing relative, and, upon further skulduggery, discovers that her name was Eileen McDonald. She had never known her name, and still doesn't know how they are related, if they ever really were.

It's a great trove of material, notes to a small, sad life, and Katz hopes to write about it one day. But Katz writes less and less often, in part because—no surprise here—the house is haunted. She doesn't believe in spirits or ghosts or an afterlife of any kind, so in the beginning she was having trouble understanding what was going on. How to explain the screwdriver that kept finding its way under her pillow, and why: was it a message? Were her screws loose? And how from time to time she'd catch a faint whiff of her mother's American Spirits (yellow box), or a to-do list in the trash can, one she was sure she had set on the kitchen counter: her mom was not a fan of "things to do." So: ha ha, Mom and Dad. The ailing relative is there too, of course, wandering around like a lost child. Katz continues to insist that she does not believe in ghosts but has decided it's not necessary to believe in ghosts for ghosts to exist; in fact, she doesn't think it's necessary to believe in anything at all. Things are or they aren't whether she believes in them or not; the rest is pure invention. The falling-icicle family fable, for instance, the seminal event in her life, the one that turned her into a writer—that happened? Really? *Please*. Not in a million years. Her origin story is bullshit. Whatever.

Time continues to pass. Eventually she publishes another book. Maybe it's this one. She could never say what she expected from her books, but they were always vaguely disappointing to her, like promising children with unfulfilled potential. At some point her parents disappear, moving on to wherever their next stop may be, but not Eileen. Eileen is still here. Her gaunt and gauzy figure, weathered face, her thin, silver hair, her pleasant but somewhat distant demeanor now reside in a chair beside Katz's bed in the Bedroom of Death, mottled hands folded in her lap, just watching her, or watching over her, perhaps. From time to time each woman reaches out for the other, but neither can touch, neither can feel. *This*, Katz writes early on, *is what one calls a formal haunting*, but upon further reflection she realizes that's not it at all. It's more that, like all the living and the dead, Eileen just wants to be with one of her own kind.

ACKNOWLEDGMENTS

I would like to thank the editors and their staffs for publishing the following stories:

Carolina Quarterly: "Welcome to Monroe"

Five Points: "[Dust Jacket Notes, Unrevised]"

Inch: "Always," "How to Build a Coffin," "Snow"

Long Story Short: "Laura, Linda, Sweetie Pie"

Pinestraw: "Gone," "*Mending Fences*: The Movie," "A
   Walk on the Beach," "First In, Last Out" (formerly
   "The End of the World")

Shenandoah: "A Night Like This"

Short Edition: "The Big Curve," "Drunk, I Kissed Her,"
   "Forever," "The Men in the Woods"

Unstuck: "Cassie"

Some of these stories were collected in a volume edited and designed by Lincoln Park Performing Arts Charter School, BatCat Press, in Midland, Pennsylvania. Thank you all so much! I loved working with you.

And love to Laura, the longest story, and the best one.

ABOUT THE AUTHOR

Daniel Wallace is the author of six novels, including *Big Fish*, his first, published in 1998, and *Extraordinary Adventures*, in 2017. In 2003 *Big Fish* was adapted and released as a movie by Tim Burton and then in 2013 a Broadway musical directed by Susan Stroheim. His novels and stories have been translated into many languages. His children's book, for which he did both the words and the pictures, is called *The Cat's Pajamas*, and it is absolutely adorable. His most recent book, a memoir entitled *This Isn't Going to End Well*, was published by Algonquin Books in 2023. He is the J. Ross MacDonald Distinguished Professor of English at the University of North Carolina at Chapel Hill, his alma mater, where he lives with Laura, his wife.